I0679911

The Secret Island Lost in Time

a novel by

Arthur Sharenow

author of
37 Summers: My Years as a Camp Director (autobiography)
and The Summer Camp Uprising (novel)

Zorba Press
Ithaca, New York USA
https://zorbapress.com/

ISBN: 9780927379571

Book cover design by Susan Krevlin
Copyediting, interior layout, and ebooks by Zorba Editing:
https://ZorbaEditing.com

For more information about this book
contact the publisher by email: books@zorbapress.com

Release date: 2024-February-22

Printed and bound in the United States of America
Printings: silit-inp-009, silit-cov-001
0102030405060708091011121314151617181920

Published by Zorba Press in Ithaca, New York, USA
https://ZorbaPress.com

Every journey
has secret destinations
of which the traveler is unaware.

— Martin Buber

Characters in the Novel, Part 1

Ellen

John & Rachel Johnson Family
      Son Carl & his wife Nancy
      Daughter Zoey & husband Hank Blake
            Children Stevie & Emily
            Children Janice and Mark

Gunnar & Amie Svenson Family
      Daughter Stacey
      Son Gunnar Junior
            Daughter Lisa

Harry & Sally Pollard Family
      Son Alan
            Son James & Daughter Grace

Malcom & Jill Abrams Family
      Son Jack & Daughter Sandy twins

Sam & Margery Westfall Family
      Sons Richie and Joe

Joe & Sally Brownstein
      Son Jimmy

Chapter 1
John's Story

Getaway Island

"Let's go everyone! We have a long ride ahead, and I want to get there before dark."

I had already described this great unchartered island off the coast of Maine to my family in amazing detail. I could not for the life of me recall how I heard about Getaway Island. I must have pictured It in a dream. The pictures in my mind were remarkably vivid. I could see our children, barefoot, running down to the water's edge, steaming cauldrons filled with lobsters, happy families waiting at nearby tables, myself lying on a hammock strung between two gorgeous birch trees, reading the Sunday sports pages. When Rachel or I inquired whether friends had heard of Getaway Island we were met with polite negatives from some, to incredulity by others who looked at us as though we had lost our minds. Many helpfully suggested alternate islands off the coast of Maine on which we could get away, islands that were on the map. Getaway Island did not exist on the most detailed maps I could find.

Rachel, who was usually willing to try anything, began to question. "John, this doesn't make sense to me; getting the whole family packed and ready to go to a place that isn't on a map, a place nobody has ever heard of and is not mentioned in any of the Maine tour books?"

"Trust me. The island exists and it's everything I say it is. When we get there we'll enjoy two-weeks just like living in Paradise. We just have to find it. I'm confident, but I understand your skepticism so I promise you, if we fail to find my island in a reasonable time, say a day or two, we'll drive further up the coast and find a vacation rental in Camden or Rockport, where there are lots of B & Bs and hotels. No matter what, we will have a great family vacation."

Boothbay Harbor was my target area. I was sure I would find my island somewhere on the Maine coast near there. The coast line there is so dotted with inlets and peninsulas and small islands, it's no wonder some of them never got noted on the maps. When we got to Boothbay Harbor, I had to settle for a space in a "No Parking zone". I didn't dare leave the car so I asked Carl and Zoey to look for a shop owner who could give us directions to Getaway Island. "They may have a different name for the island, but they should all know the bridge that connects to it. Just ask about a bridge that looks like the Golden Gate Bridge in California. It must be a local landmark. They'll all know it."

It didn't take long for them to give up. "Dad, nobody has heard of your island and nobody has seen or heard of your bridge. Are you sure this place really exists? People looked at us like we were crazy."

"Of course, it exists. Have faith. We just have to find it."

Carl whispered to his sister and made the crazy sign with his finger. I pretended not to notice or make an issue of it.

I had a good road map and had organized a search plan in my mind before we left home. After about ten hours of searching all of the likeliest side roads in the area, we were deeply into an unlikely dirt path that was so narrow pine branches were scraping both sides of the car. I was about to give up for the night and decided I would have to back out when the bushes just ahead seemed to part and the world opened up to an incredible sight. The ocean was right in front of us and there was our bridge. It looked like a small version of the famous Golden Gate Bridge, just like the picture in my head. I was not the only one excited. It was so astonishing to the kids they were shrieking. Even Rachel was giggling. My heart was filled with an unreasonable sense of joy.

"John, I can't believe it. You actually found it, and you're right. It looks just like the Golden Gate. I can't believe you were never here before. You must have been here as a kid." I just stopped the car, and the four of us looked and admired. Zoey took out her phone and insisted we take a selfie with the bridge behind us so we could have proof for our friends when we got home.

I drove onto the incredible bridge, and when we reached the high point in the middle, I stopped the car. We all got out and looked ahead. All I could see on the far side was green, an evergreen forest, starting almost at the water's edge. A narrow road seemed to lead right from the beach-head into what otherwise appeared to be an impenetrable forest. We started down off the bridge and into the inviting green curtain below. There was no sign of human habitation except the road which led into the forest. I drove slowly, not knowing exactly what I was looking for. We saw nobody, and it was starting to get dark.

The bridge was there all right, but where were the people? Where was the wonderful community I had imprinted on my brain? I started to have my doubts that we would find any human habitation, but I knew there must be. After all, somebody built a road here. I had faith we would soon come to the getaway place I saw it in my mind. I assumed the hotels and restaurants must be further in. Rachel was worrying and the kids started to grumble again as we continued without any signs of civilization. The pine forest was beautiful, and on the right there were breaks in the wall of trees and we could now occasionally get glimpses of the sea. About fifteen minutes into our drive, I spotted the first sign of life. It was literally a weathered sign. It announced "Shady Nook Resort." We followed the arrow down a narrow dirt road until we rounded a bend and saw before us a beautiful old fashioned 1920s style resort, the white siding reflecting the beautiful colors of sunset. The scene was framed by the ocean behind it.

"Wow! This looks great!" I had to stop the car and stared ahead. My heart was fluttering. It was my dream come true. My passengers were shrieking with excitement again.

A tall man wearing a Hawaiian shirt, cargo shorts and sandals came out to meet us. He looked at a clipboard and shook his head. "Sorry folks, you'll have to be going now. You're not on my list and we don't have any vacancies." I was about to ask him about other hotels in the area, but he eliminated that possibility by simply turning his back and walking away.

"Friendly sort isn't he." We were all disappointed. I think I was the most disappointed of all. "Don't worry. We'll find the place I have in my mind. It seems that was just not it."

We drove back to the main road and a few miles later Rachel spotted another sign. This one said "Happiness Inn." I turned into its dirt road, drove a short distance until we were met with the sight of a charming old stone building surrounded by a huge lawn. Again, the backdrop of the sunset across the ocean added to the appeal of the scene. In front of the building there were picnic tables filled with family groups. They were eating, chatting and some were singing.

"This is the place. I just know it. It's just the way I imagined it."

A middle-aged man got up from one of the tables and ambled toward us. He had a smiling face and a friendly look.

"Hello strangers. You look like a very nice family, just the kind of family we would like to have join us here. Unfortunately, we have no vacancies. I feel really bad about it, but I won't even be able to invite you to stay for dinner since every chair is spoken for. You must be slated to go elsewhere."

I could not believe it. What did he mean we were slated to go elsewhere? This place was almost exactly the picture I had in my head, but the man insisted they had no vacancies and not even a single place available for dinner. Again, we heard that phrase. What did it mean we were slated to go elsewhere? We got back in the car and continued on. We came to another dirt road with a sign on a tree that proclaimed "Serenity Cove." As we approached a rambling ranch style building, a whole group of men, women and children came out to meet our car. A thin middle aged woman appeared to lead the group toward us.

"There you are at last Mr. Johnson. We were starting to worry about you. You and your family are a little late for dinner, but your table is ready, and we can bring your things to your apartment to help you get settled after dinner...."

What an astonishing greeting. I was ecstatic, and could not keep the excitement out of my voice.

"Thank you. We'll be happy to join you for dinner and we would love to stay here, but you sound as though you were expecting us. How can that be? I had a premonition we would find you, but I didn't know the name Serenity Cove and I did not make a reservation. How on earth can you be expecting us?"

"You must have forgotten...or some good fairy placed the call for you. I have you down in my book. See, here's your name right here, Johnson family, party of four, a king-size bed in one room and twin beds in the other. There can be no mistake. That sounds just right for you. Now come along now and join us for dinner. I made sure we'd have all of your family's favorites for tonight."

Sure enough, there was a porterhouse steak for me, a lovely rainbow trout served under a glass dome for Rachel, hamburgers and French fries for Carl and spaghetti & zucchini for Zoey....

This was astonishing. How did they know we were coming and where did they get all information about what we all like to eat? It was truly implausible, but at the same time, it all appeared to be fulfilling the picture I had in my mind.

We unpacked that night. Our apartment, paneled throughout in a strange wood I'd never seen before, was roomy and comfortable. The kitchen and bathrooms were spacious but basic, equipped with early twentieth century appliances. Outside our apartment door were two sturdy birch trees and there was the hammock of my dreams, strung between them. The following day was one of the very best days our family has ever had. We soon discovered that all of the other residents were family groups and they were universally welcoming and friendly. There were plenty of kids around at every age and both of ours made friends at once.

We soon learned Serenity Cove was nothing like any other resort I had ever heard of. Everyone we met had been there for a very long time, and none of them seemed even the least bit concerned about when or if they would be going back where they came from. It was more like a luxurious working village than a resort. Everyone was expected to pitch in and work. I learned that most of the men worked on the farm, and some of the women too, while a few worked in the house and others were busy fishing.

On the farm they grew corn, potatoes, tomatoes, beans, carrots, and I saw they had livestock too. There were two horses, four cows and a bull. A significant area had been set aside for all aspects of poultry farming. We were also shown a woodworking shop, and, most unbelievable, a newspaper office.

In addition to the time allocated for work it was obvious from that very first day there was also time planned for recreation and socializing. More than just a village, this place seemed to be its own little world. Near the main house there was an Olympic size swimming pool, a basketball court, a horse shoe pit and, of course, swings and slides for the youngest children.

We started work early in the morning, took a brief break for lunch, and with the sounding of a loud gong all work came to an end for the day. Usually, we gathered around the pool, or sometimes on the warmest days even ventured down to the ocean. After recreation hour we headed back to our rooms and changed for cocktail hour and dinner. It's hard not to love it. Immediately, I felt this was my place.

After our first full day Zoey and Carl were so happy they thought of it as their place, just as I did. Rachel was happy, but was a little worried about what the bill might turn out to be. That was something we had never discussed with Ellen the manager.

It was not until we were ready to leave twelve days later that I learned there really was a bill to be paid, but for those two glorious weeks I just reveled in the reality that my crazy unrealistic dream turned out to be true. We were all actually living that dream. Each morning I woke up, and cautiously looked out the window, freshly energized by the reality of our new world. I was still trying to figure out how I had ever found this place and how the place really works. Is it a commune? After a few days, I stopped questioning and decided it did not matter what it was. I was prepared to just enjoy every minute of it.

I kept count of the days in my head, each day seemed to disappear in half the time of a normal day. I knew it would be hard to get back to the real world, but the calendar in my head told me I had no real choice. We had been here for twelve days and I was due back at work Monday morning.

"Kids, I hate to say it, but we've got to pack up. We're heading home tomorrow." Zoey seemed to just accept the fact, but with Carl it was another matter. He just loved the place and the life.

"No...no....no... Do we have to go? Everybody else seems to be staying on here. Nobody else even mentions going home. This is the best vacation ever. Can't we just stay?"

"I'm sorry, but we really do have to go......."

Ellen, the Serenity Cove manager, knocked on our door. "I hear you told people you are leaving. You may want to rethink that. Everybody wants you to stay and I have you booked here for the whole year. Let me show you my registry book."

"You must be joking. I had no idea we were coming. How could you book us for a year? I love it here and the kids love it here, but we have to go home and resume our real lives."

"I would not joke with you about something important. Your lives here are important and just as real as the lives you left behind. We look forward to you remaining with us for the rest of the year."

"I'm sorry, but we do have to leave. I have to get back to my job and our kids' school vacation is coming to an end. I never did ask what your rates are, but whatever it costs, it is worth it. We certainly are happy to pay for the wonderful time we have had here, and I can assure you we'll recommend Serenity Cove to all of our friends. You and this resort are just wonderful. The kids have already made me promise we'll come back again next year. Please let me have our bill."

"We certainly do not want to keep you all here against your will, but I don't think you understand. People don't just come and go here. You must have noticed that the families who come really don't seem to leave. That's the way it works. Of course, you're free to drive out of here. The entire island is at your disposal. But as for actually leaving the island I'm afraid you are in for a surprise. Leaving might turn out to be a bit more challenging than you imagine. In case you decide to return, which I sincerely hope will be the case, we'll have your apartment aired out and ready for your return. I'll have a surprise for you when you come back."

I was uneasy with the way the conversation with Ellen went. I told her we would not be back until the following summer. She gave me a broad smile and said, "We'll see. You may just be back sooner than you think." It was pretty strange that she refused to give me a bill. Perhaps the corporate office would mail it to us at home? As for a surprise when we returned, the whole place had been a surprise, quite a wonderful one in fact. I went back to our apartment and joined Rachel who had already started to pack. I wondered if we could leave some of our summer things stored here for the following year.

The next morning, we said our goodbyes to our new friends. They all seemed astonished when we told them we were leaving. Our friends, Gunnar and Amie and Harry and Sally, told us we should reconsider. They repeated what I had heard earlier from Ellen. "Nobody really leaves here." They are nice people and they meant well, but there is such a thing as reality, and it was time for us to go.

We packed up the car, and headed out of the long dirt road to the island's circumferential road, back the way we came. It was quite a silent ride. None of us was happy to be leaving. I drove for what seemed a longer time than I remembered getting back to the place where we had come over the bridge, but when we got there the bridge was gone. There was no sign of the bridge. I couldn't figure out how I could have missed it. We were right at the water's edge and the bridge was simply not there. Dumbfounded, we all got out of the car, peering into the water as though we expected to find the bridge emerging from its depths.

Then something else struck me. "Rachel, look out across the water. It's not just the bridge that is missing. The whole coast of Maine is missing! It was just a short ride over from the mainland. Take a look across. We should be able to see something. There is nothing out there but water! I don't see the bridge and the Maine coast is a very long way off. I must have turned the wrong way when we left Serenity Cove. I could swear I started back the way we came. I must have missed a turn somewhere. We'll have to backtrack until we find it."

We piled back in the car and drove back the way we came. It was completely puzzling. I was sure I hadn't made a mistake when we left Serenity Cove. When we passed the sign for Shady Nook that proved it. Then we passed the sign for Happiness Inn, and soon after that we were back at the entrance road to Serenity Cove. I resisted the temptation to drive in. I couldn't make sense of what seemed to be happening to us. The only theory I could come up with to try to justify the facts as we now knew them was that our whole island was floating; that it was not anchored in one place, but was pushed back and forth by the changing tides. I'm not sure I really believed this explanation. At least it gave me some reason to think we would be able to get off the island and back home. We simply had to look out from all different areas of the island until we caught sight of the coast of Maine. Then we would soon find our bridge.

I continued driving away from Serenity Cove, hoping that the opposite end of the island would give us a view of the Maine coast. We passed signs for two more resorts beyond Serenity Cove. I drove by them and just kept going. My hopes were dashed when the road just ended with nothing ahead of us but a forest of pines. There was nothing to do but turn around again. I could see Rachel was getting more and more upset. Her lips were tight together and she had a frozen expression on her face, but loyally she said nothing. Carl was not so circumspect.

"Dad this is crazy! Why don't we just go back to Serenity

Cove? This riding around isn't getting us anywhere. What's the point of going back across the whole island again?"

"You may be right, Carl, but I'm just going to stop at one of the other resorts and see if they can give us some kind of answer to the location of the bridge to Maine. If they can't help, I suppose we have no alternative but to return to the Cove. I started back, and stopped at the first resort we came to, a place called "Thirty Pines." I planned to ask directions or to use their telephone if they had one. The place looked much like Happiness Inn, the first resort we had stopped at the day we came. It really looked the same. I could see the ocean on the far side of their athletic field.

I wasn't surprised when we were met as we drove in. The man who came to meet us was a dead ringer for the guy who turned us away at Happiness Inn two weeks ago. "I'm sorry, I cannot help you. We don't have you booked here. You must belong to some other resort."

"Yes...You're right. We belong to Serenity Cove."

"Then why are you here? Go back to your place. Ellen is the manager there and certainly she knows everything about this island as well as I do. She will give you whatever directions you may want. By now, I assume you understand that nobody leaves our island. This island is paradise. Why would anyone ever want to leave?"

I did not like the sound of that. He made it sound as though we were all prisoners. I was not about to accept what he said as the gospel. It wasn't logical. It made no sense to me! There had to be a way off the island. I thought we had just better keep driving and eventually we would stumble onto some unlikely looking path or road that would take us to the bridge just as we had stumbled onto the road that led us to the bridge two weeks earlier. Rachel and the kids were frustrated and grumbling that they were hungry. It was a long time since breakfast. It was clear to me they were scared and ready to quit and return to our comfortable nook at Serenity Cove.

I was not. I reminded them how skeptical they all were about ever finding the bridge or the island when we first started looking and how unlikely it seemed we would ever find it, but we did. We're here. "I found that bridge once and I'm going to find it again. There is no way that bridge could have just disappeared! There has to be a logical answer somehow and I am determined to find the solution. I have no idea how it could have moved or if the island itself moved in some strange way, but we're going to find the bridge and return home." I could tell they were all furious with me now

Over the next couple of hours, I drove very slowly, turning in at every break in the forest, every break that might be a road, the road that would lead us back to our Golden Gate Bridge and home. Most of the breaks in the forest turned out to be animal paths. At some, it was not possible to drive in at all, just turning the car toward the clearing in the trees and then backing out. Some breaks in the woody landscape were so slight I could only stop and peer into the forest from the road. I checked my watch. We had been on the road now for about six hours of fruitless searching. We were running out of gas. Soon it would not be a matter of choice. I would have to stop.

My three passengers were relieved when I admitted defeat and said we were heading back to Serenity Cove. Rachel could tell how disappointed and frustrated I was. Without a word, she slid over and kissed my cheek. I could see she looked relieved.

Zoey was always the worrier in the family, "Daddy, are we prisoners on this island? Will we ever get off? I Like it here, but I miss TV and all of my friends from the neighborhood. There has to be a way to get home!"

"Don't worry. We're not prisoners. I'll figure out how to get us home, but I guess today we had just better get back to the Cove. It won't be so bad to stay for an extra day or two." That's what I said. I was beginning to wonder whether it was true.

As we drove back into The Cove the entire community was outside to welcome us home. It was as though they were waiting for us. They cheered as I pulled into the parking space next to our apartment. The children couldn't wait. They opened the back doors and jumped out with a kind of comic joy. Rachel and I sat looking at one another for a moment. Then slowly we started out of the car. Ellen greeted us with a big smile on her face.

"Ah, there you are. Everyone is so glad to see you back safely. I was hoping you would return in time for dinner... Now here you are, nice and early. You'll all have time for a swim and cocktails before dinner."

I was annoyed at her for the very first time. She was treating our painful six-hour jaunt as though we had just gone on a fun family outing. "Ellen, enough is enough! We love you and we love the place, but Rachel and I do have to get home. You have to be straight with us. How do we get out of here? How do we get home?""

"You don't really want to do that, do you? There really is no way off this island. I tried to tell you. I knew you would ultimately have to learn for yourself. It seems almost magical that from time-to-time new people find us, just like you did two weeks ago, however nobody really leaves the island and certainly nobody has ever left Serenity Cove. It is the very best place to be. I told you I had your family booked for the whole year. That was a little fib on my part. Come to the office with me. I'll show you the registry. You'll see. I actually have all of you booked for the rest of your lives, and I know you will continue to be happy here. I'm not holding you here. There is no conspiracy. The island itself is holding all of us from ever leaving. We at Serenity Cove are very fortunate. We are located on the very best part of the island, and it is up to each of us to make our lives here as fulfilling and pleasant as humanly possible. I think we do a good job of it. What do you think?"

I was speechless. She continued, "I thought it was a very nice gesture when you handed me money for your bill as you were leaving. I knew you didn't understand that nothing was owed and you would be returning so soon. I thought by now you would have noticed that money is of no use to us here. There is nothing for sale and nothing to buy. Money is pretty useless, although I do appreciate the thought on your part. Our Serenity Cove members make or grow everything we ever need. This is your home now. You insisted on going for a ride with your family today, and by now I'm sure you do understand. The important thing is that you have all returned home safely."

I was furious with Ellen. I thought we had become friends, even though we'd only lived there for two weeks. Now she tells us it is impossible to leave. Why didn't she just say that when I told her we were leaving! She let us go off on a wild goose chase, knowing full well what was going to happen when we drove away. Why didn't she tell us we wouldn't find the bridge; that we were trapped here forever!

I forced myself to suppress my anger. I didn't want to explode and have it escalate with the entire community within earshot and our kids standing nearby. I was sure I would never feel the same about Ellen as I had in the beginning; and that I would never entirely trust anything she told me. I would always wonder what she was holding back.

I had very little sleep that night and for several nights after. It was a shock to be told we were indeed prisoners. Our prison was a delightfully pleasant one, but a prison nonetheless. It took us some time to adjust to that fact.

I understood now though there was no dollar price, this was the price. We would be here forever. And yet, I started to wonder if we and the entire island were in the grip of some maniacal being. Were we being played with for some inexplicable reason? Was this really all a dream that had suddenly turned bad? I couldn't entirely believe or accept that we would be here the rest of our lives. Somewhere, somehow there had to be a way to reconnect to the real world.

Chapter 2
John

Life at The Cove

When we resumed our lives at Serenity Cove, now realizing it was not simply a vacation, we slowly started to integrate into the community, making friends and taking on responsibilities. I soon came to think of Serenity Cove as a town rather than a resort. We all had our jobs to do. Our closest family friends were The Svensons, who lived in the cabin just behind ours. They were very sociable people and had welcomed us and showed us around when we first arrived in town. They had been the most recent family to arrive before we came to The Cove, and we learned they had been here seven years. They were apparently completely at home long before we came on the scene. They originally came from Oslo, Norway, and had lived in the United States for only three years when Gunnar suddenly had a dream about this island, and, just like me, insisted to his wife Amie, that they must find the island of his dream. At the time, they were childless and relatively unencumbered. Amie didn't believe in his dream, but fell in with his "vacation" plan, their experience in getting here much like our own, miraculously finding and crossing the bridge and being welcomed as though expected at the Cove. They may have been childless when they arrived, but they quickly had three children, and Amie was pregnant with her fourth. Their son Gunnar Jr. is the same age as our twins. Carl and he soon became buddies. Their oldest girl Lisa was only a year younger than Zoey and the two of them hit it off together right away. Their baby, Kirsten, was a toddler. There were lots of babies and toddlers in the Cove. Almost every couple had one very young child. Rachel and I laughed about it when we first came, and recognized the cause. There was a complete absence of programming at night. That, together with the reality of no television, no electricity and no stockpile of contraceptives in Serenity Cove provided the answer to constant population growth for the community.

Gunnar was in charge of the Maintenance shop, and invited me to work there with him, despite the fact that I am not too handy with tools. I understood that everybody had a role to play if things were to work well, and I was happy to have something worthwhile to contribute. The shop itself was a surprise. It was a well-equipped woodworking shop, even though nobody seemed to know where the equipment came from, according to Gunnar. He and I were in charge of maintenance throughout the town. Yes, I thought of it as my town. Everybody else used the formal name Serenity Cove, which sounded a little crazy to me. I just liked the sound of "my town."

Amie introduced Rachel to a group of women whose mornings were spent homeschooling their kids. Sometimes they worked in small groups, other times with only their own children. They seemed to spend a good part of each afternoon playing Canasta or sometimes Bridge, rotating from one apartment to another. Rachel was constantly amused by Amie's disorganization. "I really love her. She's such a fun person, but what a mess! Their beds are never made and there's just stuff lying all over the place. I don't think she ever cleans. The kids' books are scattered all over the house and I can't imagine they ever learn anything with Amie as their teacher. She is just so disorganized, but such a warm and caring person I love her and so does everybody else."

Her husband was nothing like her, confirming my long-held belief that opposites attract. Gunnar was a hard worker and very precise in every task he undertook. He was the manager of the workshop and I admired his skill. He and I became friends, but it was clear from my first day in the shop, when we were on the job he was boss, a little persnickety at times, but a good guy and a very good craftsman. I really liked him.

We had also became friendly with Harry and Sally Pollard. They were a little older than Rachel and me, and had two boys, John and Alan, who were a couple of years older than Carl and Zoey. We appeared to be very compatible as couples. We often shared a table with them at dinner. Some nights we had a kind of pot luck supper for our two families. Several nights a week, there was a community dinner. The town fishermen went from table to table, depositing lobsters. Those designated as cooks each week came around with platters filled with steaming ears of corn they had boiled in the large black kettles right out there on the dining lawn. Right from our first few days in town it was apparent to us that this place was well organized and amazingly managed by Ellen and her assistants. I may have had a somewhat jaundiced view of Ellen, but I must admit she was a great organizer. Our community dinners were a perfect example of her management. There was always enough food. There were always enough places set at each table. The folks who were in charge of cleanup always did the job well and without question.

Harry Pollard ran the town newspaper, and was truly a miracle worker. His most amazing accomplishment was to have created paper, actual paper, viable for printing. He had his own secret paper-making recipe, a secret he willingly shared with absolutely anyone who agreed to listen. Considering the conditions, he had to work with, the product he produced was outstanding. He stripped the bark from the White Bark Spruce trees. As far as we knew, the White Bark Spruce only grew on this island, perhaps only in Serenity Cove. Nobody on the island had ever seen a White Bark Spruce tree anywhere else in the world before they came here. Harry was the one who gave The White Bark its name. It doesn't look like any tree anyone had ever seen before coming to the island. It certainly didn't look like a Spruce tree. From a distance, it looks like a giant oak, but its leaves appear similar to ones on Aspens and Birch trees. He explained the process to me. He would strip the bark from the trees. It could be peeled like birch bark, but was thicker and more durable. He'd soak the bark in salt water, dry it, shave it down very thin with a plane he found in the shop, and it was miraculously ready to accept ink. The White Bark Spruce was truly a remarkable tree because even after Harry skinned the lower levels, new bark regenerated almost immediately, giving him a constant source of new paper.

The fact that he had a workable press, albeit outdated, was a mystery to everyone including Harry. And if anyone was ever bothered by the mystery, they eventually let it go, just being glad for it. Just like the machinery in the workshop, he found it here when he first arrived. That amazing product plus all of the tools in the wood shop led us all to believe there was a well-developed mature society here before any of the current residents, and that entire society had disappeared. There had been much speculation about what happened to our predecessors, but the island had offered up limited clues. There were no signs of past earthquakes or destruction from hurricanes, and the only graves on the island belong to family members of present or known past residents. But the lore of Serenity Cove was that when the first of the current residents arrived everything was damp, including the insides of all of the cabins. It was generally believed that at some point in the past the island was flooded and the residents of the time must have drowned.

Ellen had lived there longer than anyone else. She said the shop, complete with equipment as well as the printing press, were there from the time she and her husband first stepped foot on the island. Harry said his printing press was rusty when he first arrived about ten years ago. It took him days of laborious scraping and cleaning to get rid of the rust. Once it was cleaned the press worked well. Speculation about who those previous people were and what happened to them was a constant source of conversation and some disquiet. If they could have vanished so completely, could that be our fate as well? Were they, like us, trapped with no way off?

Harry managed to turn out a single-sheet newspaper every couple of weeks. He was the publisher, editor and ace reporter. Our Zoey, who loved to read, asked if she could work with him on the paper. We asked him and he said, "Yes! The more the merrier, but she has to understand I take this seriously." Zoey was ecstatic. She started working on the paper two afternoons a week, and loved what she was doing. I'm not quite sure how Harry managed to find anything to write about week after week, yet somehow he does.

Harry's wife Sally, was an art collector. Fortunately, I suppressed laughter when she first told me about her collection. I thought what can she possibly collect here on the island? I grew to understand just how seriously she took her self-appointed task. Art was very popular in town. They had had a big art show once a year for years. There were several men and women who had taken up drawing and painting. Sally did neither. She meandered around the island looking for curious bits and pieces, things that caught her eye or would strike her as unusual and interesting for her collection. She put disparate pieces together, creating her own personal art. When we first walked into her apartment it was clear we were entering a treasured personal museum. Her collection defied characterization. Several pieces were actually quite striking, but others struck me as simply ugly. I'm sure nobody had ever said that to her. I certainly didn't want to be the first. Nobody wanted to be the one to hurt her feelings by telling her what they really thought of her more bizarre creations.

During our first few weeks at Serenity Cove, Rachel and Sally Pollard became close friends. They had a lot in common. Both had grown up in New York and considered themselves Big City girls. Our town was quite wonderful, yet there were times we all admitted to a yearning for our lost former lives. When discussions occasionally came up about where we all lived before we were reborn in Serenity Cove, both Rachel and Sally spoke animatedly about the years they lived in "the greatest city in the world." They raved about the excellent schools they attended, the wonderful subway system, the Broadway shows, and the endlessly interesting wonderful pastry shops, delicatessens and movie houses. I didn't exactly come from a small town, but it seemed nothing in Boston was quite as grand as its New York counterpart. Harry, who grew up in Philadelphia, didn't have much to say about his city beyond the bragging rights to the Liberty Bell and the birth of the US Constitution. Gunnar and Amie, on the other hand, were able to counter us all with descriptions of life in Oslo, which could not be duplicated in New York. Everyone in their city spoke two or three languages, they all ice skated to work six months of the year and their country produced the world's greatest skiers, proven so every four years in the Winter Olympics.

One other family became important to us. They were

already at The Cove when we arrived. Malcolm Abrams, his wife Jill, and their seventeen-year-old son Jack all had outgoing assertive personalities. Malcolm was an engineer and had started an electronics company out of his garage when he was a very young man. He had apparently struck it rich with some invention that went into every automobile manufactured everywhere in the world. He took his profit, started investing in other businesses and quickly built his own Hedge Fund. He was used to being right, and he was also accustomed to being the leader in every situation. Mal was frustrated to be in a community in which his particular skills had no real outlet. If there was one potentially negative personality in town I would point to Mal Abrams. His son Jack seemed to be a more aggressive version of himself, a chip off the old block. I know my son Carl never liked him.

Malcolm Abrams was acknowledged to be second in command to Ellen, who held the unassailable position as community leader. There were few actual contentious issues and generally his opinions were entirely reasonable. But there was something about him that convinced me he and I would never be friends. On the other hand, there was no reason we should wind up as opponents either. Rachel reported that Malcolm's wife Jill was the best player in every card group. Their son Jack liked to boss around all the teen age kids in the community. Carl and Zoey stayed as far away from him as they could because I think Jack pegged our Carl as a future rival and went out of his way to confront both of our kids over even minor things.

Chapter 3
John

How the Cove Works

Y ears passed and any thoughts or hopes we might have
had at the beginning of returning to the outside world
had long passed. Serenity Cove was our home, and we hoped it
would always be. We had grown accustomed to the missing
luxuries of the modern world, luxuries like television, movies,
hot water heaters, telephones, etc. We never gave a thought to
any of these. The one modern convenience we still had was our
family car, but there was nowhere we wanted to go we could
not get to by foot. Of course, years earlier we had tried the
radio in our Oldsmobile, but there was no hint of reception,
only static. We no longer gave a thought to any of these. We
had so much that was rewarding in our small society we would
not have changed places with anyone anywhere else in the
world.

Our family grew and changed. Carl found a wife and Zoey a
husband. They were now full-fledged members of the
community just as Rachel and I were. Ellen, the manager, was
getting older, and surprisingly, she asked me to be her assistant.
I accepted. The community was surprised. I think everyone
had assumed Malcolm would be her eventual successor as
Community leader. I was worried at the time that there would

be negative repercussions, and found it surprising when Mal didn't raise any objections to the new order. In fact, Malcolm was very cooperative whenever minor issues came along.

I helped Ellen run the place. A few months later, it became obvious to me that her health was failing. She confided to me that she was sure it was cancer and that she didn't think she had much longer to live. We talked about preparing me to take over the community when the time came. It was during that conversation when she first divulged the history that uncovered part of the magic of Serenity Cove.

"You may not have noticed, but my cabin has one extra room none of the others have."

"Everybody knows you have an extra room, we all figured it was a perk of being in charge. I've heard different theories, and a couple of people suggested that you and your husband must have added that room when you first came, before any of the current residents got here."

"John and I didn't add it. We had nothing to do with any of it. Everything was here when we first arrived. We were all alone, the only people in this entire village, and there were all of these houses sitting here, everything vacant as if waiting for people to come. It was an astonishing scene. We naturally picked the largest cabin. Most of them were damp and smelled moldy. We checked all of them, and everyone was in the same condition. It was then when we came to the conclusion that the entire village and perhaps the entire island had once been completely submerged. The fact that it was also abandoned, made us wonder if all of the people had been wiped out in a flood. I have no way to prove it, but that's what we think happened. After we settled into our cabin, the first thing we did was open all of the windows and doors in all of the cabins, bringing fresh air and light into them, hoping one day we would have company and those cabins would again be filled with life."

"Come with me. I'll show you the most important room in Serenity Cove."

I had never been in Ellen's house before. When I walked in, it appeared quite like all of the other cabins I had visited, but there was that additional room. It appeared to have been an afterthought, tacked on to the rear of the cabin. As soon as Ellen unlocked and opened the door, it was as though I had just entered into a different world. It was nothing like the rest of her cabin or any other place in Serenity Cove. It was a modern hi-tech room set up by an engineer, most likely a graduate from MIT or Cal-Tech. It was filled with electronic gadgets, large and small. There was what appeared to be a short-wave radio, dressed in World War Two olive green. Its frame appeared to be constructed of heavy-duty steel. The data plate on the lower right-hand corner proclaimed its origin was a company named Hallicrafters. Next to it stood a huge old fashioned television set, apparently made by a company named Dumont. It was a large wooden console featuring an eight-inch screen and six bulky looking control knobs. Sitting on a desk next to the enormous television console was what looked to my eyes like a crude version of a desk top computer. It had a cabinet, which housed its electronics. In front of the cabinet was a keyboard. There was no screen, nothing like a mouse and no obvious speaker system. There were several other smaller gadgets on the counter, but it was the three major ones that demanded my attention. I wondered which of them made the magic, which might connect to the outside world. I could hardly believe what I saw. It was a remarkable sight. We on the island had been living like primitives, happy well-provided-for primitives, but primitives nonetheless, and here was all of this technological hardware sitting hidden from view. To be sure, it all had to be generations out of date in terms of technology, nevertheless it sure looked modern and up to date to my eyes. It was years since I had seen anything remotely like any of the appliances I saw before me.

"Ellen, do any of these things work?" She didn't answer me directly. Instead, she had a story she wanted to tell, and was apparently determined to tell it just the way it was laid out in her mind. As if she just couldn't keep it to herself anymore after all this time.

"It was all here and it was up to John and me to figure out what to do with it. We knew that if we could get it all working we could potentially be rescued and return to civilization."

I was mystified. On the face of it, all of these relatively modern electronics were essentially museum pieces, interesting but useless artifacts from a different time and place. "How did you ever think you could make use of any of them without electricity?" In response, with a wide uncharacteristic smile and a dramatic flourish, she opened a door to a surprisingly large closet. On the floor of the closet was a Briggs & Stratton electric generator. There were two shelves above the generator each of which held a pair of five-gallon gasoline containers.

"These were also here when we arrived. My John was ecstatic when he first saw that generator. He was convinced he could get everything working and we would be able to return to the mainland. John was determined to make use of everything. He was sure he could and determined we would get it all working. He devoted all of his spare time to taking the short wave and the computer apart, airing the interiors and hand drying every single wire and tube. He then put them back together, each time convinced he could coax them back to life. He planned to send messages to the outside world using both the computer and short-wave radio for sending messages. Someone was bound to hear or see our messages and send replies which we might receive on any of the three machines. Even if our equipment couldn't receive their replies, if our messages were received, someone was bound to come looking for us. It was only a matter of time before rescuers would arrive by sea, or air."

"Although we were stranded, we loved the idea of being the only two people on our own private island. After we had been alone here for a very long time, we became spooked by the idea of being the only two people surrounded by all of these empty houses. Thank God we had each other. I'm sure you can appreciate; we felt our lives had been interrupted and we wanted to go home. John was convinced that with these three electronic marvels he would be able to reach someone and we would be rescued. As you know, that was many years ago and we never have heard from any potential rescuers. However, John's efforts succeeded in a strange and magical way neither of us could explain then, and which still defies any reasonable explanation. He activated a miracle, and the two of us took advantage of that miracle time after time to create the special society we have here today. We couldn't communicate with anyone who could rescue us; however, we could and did bring people here to join us in our world. I brought you here."

"Are you saying you actually pulled us here in some fashion?"

"Don't be shocked. You didn't just stumble on us. Through the years I have brought all of the people who live in Serenity Cove here, except the babies born here. On the other hand, I have also used the exact same procedure many other times fruitlessly as well, where the selected people never did get here. It's unclear to me why those who made it, did, or why others failed to arrive."

This was amazing information! I couldn't wait for her to reveal the secret of our town's history. Where I had been living with the idea of never knowing, I now needed to know. How did we get here? How did everybody else get here? Was the bridge real or an illusion? Were more people coming, or was it just us and our families who will give birth to future generations? What happened to the people who lived here before us? Did they leave the island or did they die here? Was there a huge graveyard somewhere on the island? Were we doomed? I had so many questions. I needed some answers, and finally Ellen was about to supply at least some of them.

"John was very cautious with his experiments. We knew the generator could create electricity, and we were able to power the machinery, but we had to be very selective in using it because every hour of use would reduce our gasoline supply. That is still a major concern, though much less important than in those early years when there were very few of us here. Right now we're down to our last five gallons. He experimented with all three machines and was finally able to bring the old computer to life. We were so happy that day. We were laughing and screaming with joy, convinced we would send out messages and would soon be on our way home.

"We sent out messages on several different broadcast bands. We didn't know where we were sending them, but we were convinced that someone would receive them, realize we were in trouble, and would contact a rescue organization to find us. John was ever the optimist. Of course, there was never any way to actually know who we reached. Every day we ran the computer for an hour or so and sent out our message. After a month without out any apparent success, we were just about to give up when we started getting undecipherable responses. They sounded like gibberish on the short wave, and looked like squiggles and odd lines on the television screen. And then the messages suddenly stopped again, and we were terribly disappointed. A few days later we heard a car on the main path. We ran out to greet the car, and it was Mal and Jill Abrams. They became our very first neighbors.

"Mal didn't remember getting any signal or message from his computer. The 'message' he received seemed out of thin air.

He didn't know how he got it. He simply woke up one day with this crazy unshakeable image of a magical island he just had to see. He knew it was off the coast of Maine and that he would get to it by crossing the Golden Gate Bridge. It obviously didn't make any sense, but he was determined to find it. And he did. He was so happy and excited to find us we swallowed our disappointment that they had not come as our rescuers. We recognized the magic of their arrival and celebrated the joy of finally having neighbors."

"His story must sound familiar to you."

"Yes, of course." My heart was pounding as I listened to an experience almost identical to our own.

"Excited to have company at last, we decided to transmit a message in which we would actually describe the island and the bridge. Then we picked a name we liked from one of the old phone books we found piled in a corner of this room and concentrated on that person's name as we sent out our message, simply typing the name on the computer. How it reached the people we chose, I have no idea, but I do know it worked. In the case of every one of our arriving families, some member of that family had this same vision and compulsion to follow it. And not one of you remembers getting any direct message from your television or radio. In the early days, no one we contacted owned or had ever used a computer. You were the first of our incoming residents who had a computer at home. As far as each of you was concerned the image and the compulsion to find us came out of the blue, with the same exact experience. This phenomenon kept repeating over and over through the years.

"In those first few years, we worked with the old computer and the short wave almost every day. Most of the time, it failed to produce any result. We went weeks and sometimes months before new people joined us. Every once in a while a new couple or family would drive in, all with the same tale, the same story you had. After the first four or five families, we experienced another unexplainable phenomenon. As all of you received messages that brought you here, I started to get messages in my head telling me who was coming and when we were to expect them. I would wake up on arrival days knowing people were coming, and what hour to expect them. I also inexplicably already knew their names and ages. I entered them all in my guest book. I would immediately share this information with the whole community, confident that all of our people would welcome the newcomers enthusiastically and help them adjust to our world as rapidly as possible. So, you see, it was just as mysterious and magical to John and me as it has been for all of you.

"All of our newcomers were thrilled when they first arrived. Quite a few expressed a degree of frustration when they realized there was no way off the island. However, that emotional period usually passed within a very few weeks. All of these years, there were only two who were seemingly terribly agitated they couldn't return home. Many years have passed and they are still with us, and have long since made peace with their life here.

"I was actually shocked when you, John, were so very

insistent about trying to get back home. You were the only one who actually packed up and made a serious effort to create a miracle of your own by taking your family and returning home. Happily, once you realized it was impossible to leave the island, you came back to us and you and your family have not only integrated into the community, you have become one of our strongest leaders.

"As unbelievable as it was to those who joined us here and became our community, it was even more incredible to John and me at first. Then, day to day living became our focus, and the rest fell away. It is only now that I am telling it all to you that I realize again how truly improbable this must all sound.

"Your family was the most recent to join us and you've been here for years now. It's time for us to start up the old computer and short-wave again. I'll work with you. We'll see if we can find another family who will come to help renew our community. I would love to be able to join you in welcoming one more new family to our community. That would give me great pleasure. I want you to replace me as leader and to be keeper of the secret, but ultimately you may decide you want to hold an election to find your successor. I wanted to avoid a political problem, so I spoke with Mal, letting him know I wanted you to be the next leader. I wasn't sure how he would take it. He surprised me. He was entirely agreeable; said you'd make a fine leader.

"Now you know everything I can tell you. It's a relief for me to finally share it, and I won't be here that much longer. I leave it up to you how far you wish to spread the information."

We both sat quietly for a while as I absorbed and tried to process so much new information. What I had just learned answered many questions, but left some unanswered. I knew it would take time for me to process and completely accept it all, including my proposed new leadership role. Ellen sat watching me for a while. Then she asked "Are you ready?" I nodded yes.

"We have phone books here from all of the cities in the Northeast. I want you to look at them and find an appropriate person to join our community here."

"Appropriate person?! How can I possibly know who will be appropriate just by looking at names in a phone book?"

"It does seem an unlikely method, but it is the one I always used. It worked for me. Don't worry, whoever you pick will be the right choice."

"But when I pick someone how will he or she know to come here?"

"The same way you knew. The same way we all knew. Nobody selected John and me. There we were, perfectly happy raising our kids in Rockville, Maryland when suddenly I had this dream. At least I thought it was a dream, and I insisted on following it. Now I know it was not a dream. There is something totally inexplicable here. It's mystical. Don't you agree?"

"You never mentioned you had children before. Did your children come with you? Where are they?"

"I never mentioned them because it kills me to think all of these years have passed with no connection between us and the sure understanding that I will never see them again. Please don't ask anything further about them. I prefer not to revive the terrible pain and awful ache that we experienced when we realized we had lost them forever. The pain is never truly erased, but with the passage of years the ache has lessened." She stopped for a minute, sniffled and looked as though she was about to cry. Then she abruptly stopped, pulled herself together and was again the calm and efficient person I had always known.

"You'll pick a person from the phone book. We will transmit the idea to a member of that family, and, if he or she is the right person, his brain will pick it up. He will feel compelled to find us, just as you were. Let me know when you have found another family you want to reach. I'm sure they will be a nice family, hopefully as nice as yours. Then we will all concentrate hard on the most likely member of that family and he or she will find a way for them to join us. If that family doesn't join us in a reasonable time period, you will select another."

"We'll start up my faithful old generator and plug in the computer and the short wave. You'll type the name and address of the family you've picked. Then we'll send our message by simply clicking "Enter." That's it. It shouldn't work but it does. The message I've sent through the years has been something like this.

Come to Getaway Island. It is the answer to your dreams. You and your family will love it. Look for the Golden Gate Bridge. Come as soon as possible."

"That's all. Then they come or they don't come. Most of

those we select never get here, but the few who do are the wonderful people who live here now."

I scanned the phonebooks for Greater Boston, Philadelphia and Baltimore. Then for no reason at all, my pen stopped at the name Brownstein, Joe Brownstein. His name was in the phonebook for Greater Boston. He and his family lived in Newton, a suburb of Boston. The message was sent. Ellen showed me how to turn off and drain the generator. Then we left her cabin and resumed all of our normal activities. We didn't tell anyone else we had issued an invitation.

Early one morning I heard a rap on our cabin door. "John, they're coming! They got the message! They'll be here tomorrow." She was so excited. That's when I told Rachel, filling her in on everything Ellen had told me including the invitation I had transmitted. We then started spreading the news and actual details to everyone. The whole community was buzzing with excitement. It had been many years since we had come to the Cove.

When the Brownsteins first pulled into the grassy area adjacent to our outdoor dining tables, we gave them a grand welcome and listened as they described the same incredible journey we had all experienced over that magical Golden Gate bridge. They were a couple, in their early forties and their children were just about the same ages as our kids had been when we first arrived. Joe and Sally Brownstein and their girls were quickly and easily integrated into the community.

Just a few months after the Brownsteins joined us, our wonderful and indispensable Ellen died. Everyone in the community mourned her passing. I think I mourned her most of all. She had passed the torch to ME. I was now the keeper of the secrets. I had the pressure of knowing that I must now take on leadership and responsibility for the whole community. I thought back to how upset I was with her when we were newcomers and had that abortive attempt to leave the island, how peculiar and unhelpful she seemed. I accepted the responsibility that had always been Ellen's and I was content that my family and I would live out our lives here in Serenity Cove, but in the background there was always the unknowable. Knowing that we'd live out our lives here, didn't make me dismiss basic questions I had. What is this mysterious magical power that allows us to attract and draw in new members? Even more important and equally unknown, what happened to those who lived here before us? Will some catastrophe overwhelm us all? Will it happen again, and in my lifetime? Time and nature were to provide the answers.

Chapter 4
John

Water Rising Crisis

At a recent residents' meeting, I was asked by one of our younger members how I came to be leader of the Cove and what I did before my family came to Serenity Cove. I told them all about how Ellen had taken me under her wing and told me the history I needed to understand so that one day I would succeed her. Before Rachel and I came here with our family I was the director of a children's summer camp. In a sense, what I did for years there was very much like what I do now.

My camp was a little like Serenity Cove. We were in a rural area, far from our campers' homes. The parents of the campers sent them to us both to enjoy life away from the city and hoping it would help them achieve a degree of independence. Our camp offered a variety of activities: sports, outdoor living, drama and various crafts all geared for boys and girls ranging from about seven years old until they were fifteen or sixteen. My responsibilities there were much greater than here. Here we are families. At our camp Rachel and I and all of our staff played the role of families for our campers as well as serving as their school and activity center.

As the person in charge, I was the one responsible for the

health and safety of everybody on our site. It was my job to make sure that every place the children lived in was safe and that every activity was safe. But, of course, it was more than that. We had instructors teaching many different kinds of skills at every age and ability level. It was my job to see that the instruction was correct and carried on in a way that was beneficial to all of our campers, that helped them grow physically and emotionally.

The contrast between what I did as a camp director and what I do here is enormous. We are all here to protect our children and all of our family. That is our primary care and responsibility. At camp where we worked the parents were far away. I had final responsibility. Here you come to me with an occasional emergency, but such situations are rare. Here I do the programming and job assignments and help make up the special activities we have on weekends, but you do the most essential job of all, that is taking care of your family. I am just here as an extra to back you all up.

Ellen did the major job years ago when she created and transformed our Cove from the empty shell she found when she first arrived into the wonderful place we enjoy now. It is my challenge to follow her lead and that is what I try to do. But I couldn't do it without all of you. Every day I thank God that my family and I were fortunate enough to be surrounded by such fine human beings who make everything I do here such a pleasure."

After I finished my response there were a few friendly questions, but everyone seemed pleased with my answer.

The days, the weeks, the months, and even the years seemed to fly by. Rachel and I were well aware we were no longer young, perhaps not even middle aged. We often stopped to reflect on our good fortune since arriving at the Cove. We both still had a share of the youthful energy we had when we first came, and I was still leading the Cove, but I knew I should get to the business of choosing a successor. Our kids have been great since we first stepped on this island. We are proud of our son Carl, who has grown into a terrific young man, a good husband and father. We loved being with him and his wife Nancy, who is a sweet and even tempered. She is a marvelous mother to Emily and Stevie. The two of them started a day camp several years ago. Our daughter Zoey hit the jackpot when she married Hank, the best all -round guy in the whole town, excepting of course for Carl. Nobody could be quite as special as him. Zoey and Hank were in charge of dining services for the community. They took charge of community dinners on Wednesday and Sunday nights. When they got married, we warned both of our kids that twins often give birth to twins, but both were relieved when their children were born one at a time. Twins would certainly have been lovely too, but having babies one at a time was much simpler for them as young parents. Zoey's son Mark was two years older than his sister Janice, and Carl's Emily was four years older than her brother Stevie.

In all of the years since our initial adjustment to the fact we could never leave, Rachel and I had a good life, a happy life at the Cove. I was content to spend the remaining years of our lives there in our own paradise until, slowly, a new reality from the outside world seemed to be encroaching. I noticed a disturbing change. At first I thought I was imagining it. It didn't take long before I became certain. I shared my observation and concern with Mal, Gunnar, and Harry and Rachel, of course. Not surprisingly, they had all noticed the same change; little by little, the water level around us was rising. Our glorious wide beach had started to recede some time ago, but I only began to notice when I saw water rising on the pillars which supported our fishing pier. The tides do ebb and swell and occasionally I deluded myself into thinking the water level was reversing again. That delusion did not last long. Part of me wanted to stay in denial. However, it wasn't long before everyone became aware that the rising of the water level was accelerating. If this trend continued we feared it would be only a matter of time before our island became uninhabitable.

The issue had to be beyond just our community. It would affect everybody on the island. Though we had little connection or contact with any of the other resorts, I knew it was time to consult with the leaders of the two resorts closest to ours. I consulted with our other long-term members, and all agreed it was imperative that we meet and plan together with our neighboring resorts.

I asked Carl to reach out to them. He took our car, which he had never before driven, and went to our closest neighbors. He reported back they were equally interested in a meeting. When we met there was no doubt. They had all observed the same threatening rise in the sea level. One fellow from

Happiness Inn claimed he measured the rise at over two feet from what had been normal. We agreed we had to figure out a way to evacuate the island should the rise water level rise continue. Bill James, the leader of Shady Nook Resort, knew more island history than we did, specifically, the mystery of the bridge. According to him, our "Golden Gate" bridge was under water and hence, invisible almost all of the time. Every so often when tides ran very low for a short window of time, the water receded around the island, and the bridge came into view. These rare and exceptionally low tides allowed the bridge to become visible and usable; but only for three or four days, and then it was like it had never been there at all.

Rachel, the kids, and I must have arrived right at the end of one of those windows, because when we had looked for it again, it was gone. Bill told us that for most of the past thirty or forty years the water level has had been too high for the bridge to be seen under normal conditions. The bridge had remained unseen, underwater , and unused for decades, and was just a myth to those who were born on the island. Every family who came across the bridge had done so on one of those rare periods when the tides were at their lowest ebb. Now, even as the trend is for a higher and higher normal sea level there will still be periods of two, three or even four days when the channel between us and the mainland will drop precipitously and the glorious "Golden Gate" bridge will reappear. Neither Bill James nor any of the rest of us could even imagine who originally built the bridge or how it came to be where it is. No one knew.

It was a productive meeting. The consensus of our community leaders was that we should take advantage of the very next low tide period, or we might miss the last chance to save all of our lives. The consensus was, that as much as we loved our island, in order to survive, the time had come to get out. We should plan to leave the very next time the bridge emerged from under water.

Each of us has agreed to post a sea watcher whose job it would be to check the sea level from observation points close to their own resorts on a regular basis. Their job would be to have immediate, first-hand knowledge of the water level so they could alert their communities when the tide appeared to be nearing the level at which the bridge should reappear. According to the plan, that would be our collective signal to pack our cars and head to where we originally crossed the bridge. We all agreed cars should be started up a couple of times a week to make sure they'd run. And should be packed with anything important in advance. We would then wait there for the bridge to fully emerge, and when it did we would drive across to the Maine coast, and safety.

After that meeting, we all started to pay close attention to the tides. It seemed obvious that what must have happened to those who had occupied Serenity Cove and the other occupied areas on the island at the time. Those poor souls had built their buildings, brought their equipment and lived their lives here a good many years before the deluge came that wiped them out, and well before any of us had followed the dreams that led us to the island. When the seas rose, it must have completely swallowed the island, drowning all of its inhabitants before they could escape. If any of them had made it out alive their story would have made the papers and news on the radio, achieving a degree of notoriety. The island itself would have become well known, if not actually famous. There had apparently been no survivors to tell the tale. I was convinced that's what happened, and it now was my responsibility to somehow prevent my family and friends from coming to the same unimaginably ghastly end.

It had been important to discuss it with the leaders of the other communities, and to see if we could agree on a plan of action. The plan we came up with sounded feasible, but after the meeting, I began to have serious reservations. I started imagining all that could go wrong; and the more I thought about it, the more I visualized a disaster. The main issue would be too many of us would be in too narrow an escape route. I pictured a massive traffic jam. The first few cars to get to the bridge might well be fine. They would get to it, and be able to cross over, but after they crossed they would only be able to move very slowly along that terribly narrow pathway, more dirt path than actual roadway, until they finally reached modern paved roads and could start to move more briskly. Even if all went well and there were no break-downs there would be an enormously long backup. There would certainly be a number of cars from all of the resorts on the island. I foresaw cars stalled on the bridge as the waters started their inevitable rise. Behind them on shore a long line of cars would never even reach the bridge, and would be swallowed by the rising seas. It is also possible that one of the very old cars could break down completely blocking the line of cars behind it.

While mulling it over my sentiment shifted from doubting the efficacy of the plan, to a certainty that it would prove to be a catastrophe for us. Since Serenity Cove was geographically the third-closest community distant from the bridge, if we were to follow the plan and started toward the bridge on the day we got the signal from our sea watchers, our cars might not even get to the bridge under any likely scenario. We would drown in our cars, in the rising tide.

It was clear to me that we had to devise a different plan for Serenity Cove members which would get us to the mainland before anyone else. In order to survive, we have to start out before the others, which meant before the bridge became visible.

There had to be a solution.

One night I woke out of a sound sleep and the answer came to me! I jotted it down on the pad next to the bed. When I woke up the next morning, I found the answer to our salvation scribbled on a small square of note paper.

I intended to call a town meeting and describe my plan. Then I talked about it with Rachel to see what she thought of my idea.

John, it's a sensible plan, but do you want to just announce this to everyone? Don't you think you want to get a few key people behind your plan to assure success before you spring it on everyone at the meeting?"

There were times when I wished Ellen was still alive. I'd

have loved to be able to talk to her about the whole situation over with her, but she'd been gone for years by then. Because the decision to put this idea to a town meeting was fully mine, I did have to get clear on how I wanted to present everything. I needed to consult with Gunnar, who was still head of the shop and town maintenance, my son Carl, who had developed into a first-rate carpenter and had long since replaced me as Gunnar's assistant, and with Harry, our resident expert on the vital White Bark Spruce trees.

We met in the workshop. I told them about my meeting with the leaders of the other communities and about the plan that had been reached. Then I told them about my reservations, and waited for them to give their opinions. I told them what I had in mind.

"What do you think about the possibility of building rafts strong and sturdy enough to carry us and our most important belongings to safety? Is this a pipe dream? Is it possible?"

Gunnar was the first to respond; and the others naturally looked to him for leadership in anything that involved construction. "I don't know, John. We would have to build a lot of small rafts to transport all of us and our belongings. Assuming we could build them, we would still have to figure out how to get the rafts from here to the shore closest to the mainland coast." I could see from his expression his mind was busy working through the problem.

"I don't know. There are a lot of variables and unanswered questions. I'm guessing most people would feel a whole lot safer relying on their cars making it across the bridge than having to depend on rafts that do not exist yet. But yes, I suppose we could build them if we have enough time and everyone agrees that this is what we want to do."

Harry was far more enthusiastic and very positive about the project, excited even. As our tree expert, he assured us the white bark spruce wood is very strong and could be made to hold tremendous weight. And, he believed the bark could be shaved down and would be flexible enough to make sails to use in case wind was a factor.

Over the years we have had a few town meetings, but this was the first in which every member of the community came, from the very oldest to toddlers. It was hardly a surprise. Since the threat was now universally recognized, there was a prevailing sense of fear palpable throughout Serenity Cove, and all of the island.

I started by telling everyone about my meeting with the other resorts, and how I realized that we needed to do this on our own, in our own way, given our distance from the bridge. I filled them in on all my internal conversations, and how I came to the plan for us to evacuate the island, defeat the elements and reach the mainland! Then I had to really sell it. I knew there'd be questions, resistance, worry. When I outlined my plan, I asked for comments.

Mal strenuously disagreed. John, your plan sounds plausible, nobody can question that. BUT, it depends on too much that's unproven. I know Gunnar says we can build rafts that will hold us, and even rafts that will hold our cars, which I can't really picture, but what if he's wrong? And Harry says he can make sails from the bark of the White Bark Spruce, but what if those sails can't hold up against actual strong wind? There are a lot of ifs. On the other hand, I know we can count on our cars. They may be old, but we can make sure they all have enough gas in them to get us across the bridge and back to civilization and we know they can hold us and as much stuff each family wants to bring with them. I hate to think of abandoning everything we have accumulated here just to get on a raft which may or may not carry us to safety."

I watched their faces trying to read their reactions to Mal's concerns. Then I was ready with my reply. "All of your concerns are reasonable, but it is not my idea to rely primarily on the rafts, but to have them as a backup in case there are too many cars and too little road. To me the most important point is to get there before anybody else, to get as many of us as possible across the bridge, hopefully all of us, and to use the rafts as a backup." The discussion went back and forth for a while. It was plain, everyone was worried and some were scared, but they had relied on my leadership over the past two decades. Despite their fears and reservations, they gave me a vote of confidence, voting for my proposal. And to be honest, what choice did they have? They wanted and needed to believe in my solution.

Then we immediately got into action. It was an incredible sight to see, so many people working day after day, working as hard and quickly as possible to make it happen. Carl was in charge of the group clearing the forested area nearest to where the bridge had been. Hi job was to make it into a parking lot.

This meant that he, and the three young men he recruited to work with him, left home with a variety of tools to help them clear the land and smooth the ground surface. We had estimated it would take four or five days of intense labor. The resulting lot would have to be large enough to hold a dozen cars, and still be invisible to any who might pass nearby before we were ready to put it to use.

Harry was in charge of the White Bark Spruce project. He instructed his group of six young men and women how to strip bark off the trees. This was painstaking and highly skilled work, as they had to shave it off without tearing it. As soon as a tree was stripped, we could see the bark start to regenerate almost immediately. It never ceased to amaze. The result was a seemingly endless supply of the precise material we counted on to be strong enough and flexible enough to become the sails our rafts would need.

Gunnar had two working groups. The first was in charge of using the old wood shaving planes in his shop to reduce the stripped bark into sheets thin enough and yet strong enough to become our sails. The second group functioned like lumberjacks, busy sawing down selected trees and cutting them into logs. The logs were first planed flat on one surface and then bound together to create the many rafts we were counting on. At the very beginning of the process, we were stunned to discover another gift from the incredible White Bark Spruce. As soon as a tree was cut down, a new young one emerged from one of its roots, and immediately started growing at an incredibly rapid rate, as if to fill a quota. This gave a potentially unlimited supply of logs for the future, if there was to be a future on the island. So, it appeared we had the materials we needed. Our only real limitation would be the time and energy required by our various crews of amateur builders. It remained to be seen if we could get it all done in time.

Our plan was to get the rafts built, have a sail for each raft, and use long narrow branches as masts. We were approaching what we had started calling D-Day. The seaside parking area was nearly complete, and we were getting ready to transport the rafts on top of the cars from the town to the lot. We would move the cars late at night so as not to attract the attention of the other communities which lay between us and our takeoff point. At the parking area, we'd stack the rafts, leaving room to park just a few cars. Each family was to pack up and transport the things they wanted to take with them, to a designated storage section in the lot. On D-Day Minus One, we would pack as many people as possible into as few cars as necessary , move to the staging area, and get the rafts into position at water's edge, ready to take off at daybreak. We would load a few empty cars onto the most sturdily built of our rafts for use while the rest of us paddled or sailed to the mainland on the smaller rafts. Once we were safely across, at we'd get in those few vehicles and drive to the first town we encounter. All of this had to be accomplished between the time the sea level became low enough to see the highest point of the bridge, but before it actually fully emerged, at which time it is safe to assume all of the other communities would be starting their car caravans toward the bridge. That was the objective. We had to beat them all to the mainland on our rafts, drive our cars off the rafts and head back to Boothbay Harbor. Our work crews worked feverishly to complete our construction work and be ready to go when our sea watcher told us the time had come. Departure Day was looked upon with hope and fear, hope we could get back to the mainland and fear that our carefully designed scheme might end in disaster. I must admit I shared both the optimism and the fear.

Chapter 5
John

The Getaway

A few months later, our sea watcher told us the time had come. We alerted our families, and everyone readied themselves to move on signal. We had all been preparing ourselves on a number of levels, and as soon as the word came, with tears flowing from almost every eye, we packed our final few items and left our homes, which held so many happy memories, behind, and headed toward the bridge.

As we neared the takeoff point I could see the top of the superstructure of the Golden Gate Bridge. The lower part of the bridge was still hidden. Our timing appeared to be perfect. The other communities would all be getting notice tomorrow morning and their caravans would start. We loaded our rafts as soon as we got to our parking area. It was our plan to be paddling across onto the mainland before any of the others even reached the bridge.

Our staging area was buzzing with activity pre-dawn the next morning. Unfortunately, it was a stormy morning, with sheets of rain pouring down and high winds complicating all of our efforts. It took more manpower, and more time than any of us anticipated to load the five cars we were to float across on their sturdy rafts. Each of these rafts was operated by one volunteer driver. We recognized the real possibility that the weight of the cars might prove to be too much for our homemade rafts. We had more optimism about the rafts that were to carry only people. I anxiously watched as our auto-laden rafts started floating away toward the mainland. As soon as they started moving, we got busy again on our side, moving the remaining rafts to the water's edge.

Early that morning, we were in position, ready to board and go. This was our long- planned D-Day. This was the promised return to the mainland and safety. Then, two alarming things happened simultaneously. Without warning, huge waves swept toward those of us still on land, and toward our rafts which already were carrying the cars. The rafts started to flounder. One of them had already tipped into the water with car and driver already invisible behind the growing waves. The sky was suddenly dark and there were flashes of lightning. Right at the very same moment, I heard and then saw the caravan of cars coming from Shady Nook, our closest neighboring community.. Even though the road surface of the bridge was still under water, they attempted to drive across. As we watched their first cars started onto the bridge. We could see the water level rising as their cars moved farther along the bridge. The first two of their cars seemed to stall; and then they were simply swept off the side of the bridge by an incoming wave. They sank out of sight as we stood there mesmerized and helpless as at least ten of the Shady Nook cars disappeared into the waves. Each of those cars had been filled with people. I wondered if any of them could possibly survive.

I turned my attention across the water toward the mainland where our five reenforced car rafts had been headed. The first two cars had floated off their rafts and disappeared. The relatives of the drowning drivers cried out in horror and despair. Even the most distraught among them realized there was no time for mourning. The water level was rising fast around us. We did not have to push our rafts into the water, the water was already under and around us. Hoping for the best, we climbed onboard. Our raft had our whole family, Rachel, Carl, his wife Nancy and their children, and Zoey, Hank and their kids. All of us had paddles and we were able to get our sail up. We were moving and staying afloat, but we could not direct our movement. It was impossible to actually steer toward the opposite shore. The waves were enormous, and growing larger. Seconds after we started moving, I couldn't see anything but water. All of our other rafts were at that moment invisible to us behind the huge and disorienting waves.

After what felt like about an hour, there was a momentary lull. I looked up and saw that miraculously, several of our rafts were nearby, being driven more by the wind and waves than by the efforts of the occupants, all of whom were paddling furiously. Looking back toward the island, I was able to see the bridge now, almost fully emerged above the water. There were no cars on it. Nor was there any evidence of human movement on what had been the shore. The cars from Shady Nook which we had last seen in line near the takeoff point had been swamped and were completely under water. It hit me that we were the only survivors.

We were afloat, but apparently powerless to direct where we were going, and seemed to be moving out to sea. Our rafts were being controlled by the strength of the tide. An hour later, our island was barely visible in the distance. Much of the island was already under water. We had escaped just in time, but escaped to what and where? How many of our friends didn't make it? Had we really escaped or just changed our location, doomed to die in some other watery grave?

Some time later, although we were still getting tossed around by the sea, it was not as violent as it had been earlier, and for the few of us who were still afloat, it was possible to steer towards one another. We got close enough to shout back and forth to one another. There were only five rafts left afloat, with an average of nine to ten people in each raft. Daylight was disappearing, but off in the distance we could make up the silhouette of another island. I felt heavy with the responsibility for all of the lives that had been lost, and continued responsibility for those of us who had made it so far. We had to get to the target island before it was totally dark and to be able to find a safe landing place. Exhausted as we were, we mustered the strength and determination to paddle towards the darkening silhouette. As we drew closer the island it did not look at all welcoming, it seemed to be a series of jagged mountain peaks emerging from the ocean, all unfriendly looking rocks and ledges. Here and there, bushes and small trees peaked through, softening what would otherwise be totally untenable as a place to land. The seas, though they had calmed some, were still powerful enough to make controlling our direction very difficult. Somehow, we located a small beachhead and dragged ourselves out of the ocean.

We were exhausted and soaked from battling the wind and waves, but exhilarated to have escaped and by the knowledge that so many of us had been able to make it out alive and together. Few though we were, we were still a community. I knew it was my job to convert this unlikely, inhospitable spit of land into our new home. Those were my last thoughts as I collapsed on the beach and allowed myself to give in to exhaustion.

Chapter 6
Carl's Story

A New Home?

When I opened my eyes, the sun was dazzling, lighting up the cliffs so they shimmered with promise, rather than the ominous threat of danger we saw as we approached the island the day before. The lustrous blue sky was enhanced by occasional fluffy fair-weather clouds. The white sand beach glistened in the sun, while the sea itself, so angry yesterday, rose and fell gently. What a gorgeous day! It was hard to believe this scene after yesterday's nightmare battle through the turbulence of the rising sea. The idea of a day to relax and recoup our strength while reveling in the brilliance of the day was so inviting. I marveled at our miraculous deliverance from yesterday's struggle, turmoil, devastation and death.

With the sun on my back, I felt grateful, and so very sad. The elation of having survived such an ordeal, and the glory of being alive faded as my thoughts shifted to the almost certain death of so many of our friends from Serenity Cove. The image of that scene on the beach and the bridge, the water rising and the cars sinking out of sight beneath the waves, was seared into my brain. Was it possible that any of them made it? Did any of them reach the mainland? It seemed inconceivable, and the thought they must all have drowned was excruciating.

What a horrible way to die! I sat stunned by the horror, tears flowing down my face. I sat that way for a while, mourning their loss.

After a time, I got focused on what we had to do next. We would have to take action, even while processing what had happened. The current situation called for sustained effort by everyone who was physically able. We had to keep going, working and working as fast.

I didn't want to presume to be the one in charge, but Dad was clearly exhausted from yesterday's enormous battle for survival. He had been our leader all of my life, but he was in no condition to lead now. Mom and Dad were both stretched out on the beach sound asleep. We couldn't wait for him and our other older leaders to regain their strength. Survival depended on someone taking charge and getting us organized right away or there might not be a future.

The treasured possessions of each of us, which we had saved when we left Serenity Cove, were either strewn on the beach or floating gently in the water. We had to get them from the water-logged rafts onto the sliver of beach before they floated away or sank out of sight.

It had been difficult to predict what we would need when we packed and now there was still no way to know which of the our belongings would be important or valuable, but for now we had to salvage everything possible.

Our beach was about two hundred yards from one side to the other, a perilously narrow strip, as narrow as ten yards from the edge of the water to the base of the towering cliffs.

Somehow we had to get to a place that promised genuine safety?

Nancy and Zoey had started stretching the remains of our ragged sails between trees, creating a makeshift shelter against a possible future storm. Everybody else was either stretched out on the beach, too tired to move, or waist deep in the water rescuing everything they could from the rafts. The rafts themselves were in bad shape, having smashed against jagged rocks as we landed yesterday. That was quite a landing. We all suffered bangs and bruises, but fortunately nobody was gravely injured. Our rafts had been packed with everything we could not bear to leave behind as we fled Getaway Island. Even though three of the rafts broke up completely as we crashed into the rocks, we succeeded in keeping many of the our belongings from sinking out of sight or floating away. Everything was, of course, water-logged, but we hoped the heat of the sun which baked the beach would be able to dry most of the items, making them salvageable.

I felt sure there had to be more to this island than this tiny beach and the threatening cliffs which loomed above us. I doubted we were safe here. The water level was low, but would rise and when that happened, even a few feet higher might cause the entire beach to disappear. Obviously, we couldn't stay put. We were going to have to search and find a more permanent place to live, if there was one. It seemed like nobody else was interested in taking over leadership; so, I decided I would at least until Dad was ready to resume control.

I went over to the side of the beach where all the young

people were organizing what was still in good shape, and sorting trash from treasure, etc. "Hey guys, time to take a break. I think we need a meeting to figure out where we stand and what the possibilities might be on this island." Slowly they made their way onto the beach, many of them still dragging precious items they had salvaged. Nancy and Zoey kept working, trying to create a temporary canvas shelter. We all gathered close to them.

"It's clear we cannot can't count on staying on this beach for very long. We're going to have to get over or around those cliffs. Unfortunately, none of us is an experienced climber. At home, it was so flat nobody ever had to climb anywhere. There were no mountains, not even sizable hills. Experienced or not, someone's going to have to climb. I'm ready, but I need somebody to come with me. Whoever does the climbing will need support or a spotter, it's definitely going to be dangerous. It'll be a whole lot safer if there are two or three of us working together."

They were all gathered around, some plopped down on the sand, others stood, happy for the chance to just relax a bit. Once they quieted down, I started to tell them what I thought we should do.

"I want to see if there's a route around or through those cliffs. We need to find out what we're up against. We have no idea how large or what kind of land this is. There could be nothing on the other side but rocks! Hopefully it will turn out to be large enough and fertile enough for us to not only survive, but to settle and create a new version of Serenity Cove.

That is not what we were shooting for when we left home. We expected to get to the mainland, so this is a huge change. But we must all face the new reality. Some day in the future we may get back to the mainland, but for now we must shoot for a safe future. What I do know is, we can't survive long on this beach. We have to watch the tides, but it seems it wouldn't take much of a wave to swamp it completely. We have to locate land high enough above sea level for us to build houses and grow food." I was going to tell them I was ready to lead an expedition to attack those cliffs, but Gunner Jr., my oldest and most reliable friend, interrupted.

"Yeah, that makes sense, Carl. We all agree that's what we hope to find, but what do we do if there's no good land here? We can't just wait while people go looking. We should have a backup plan as well. I think some of us should start right away, salvaging the logs from our rafts while a small group continues sewing our sails back together. I know we don't have enough of those logs to make six rafts again, but we should be able to make at least three decent rafts, possibly four ready to sail, and maybe we can sail around the island to see what's possible. That might actually be the best way to explore the rest of this the island. But if the prevailing wind takes us in another direction, maybe we'll be luckier this time and sail to some place where there is civilization. Then we can get the coast guard to come back and find the rest of you. Like I said, I'm pretty sure, with some help from my dad and a few others, I can get at least three of our rafts refitted so they can sail again. If nothing else, that would give about twenty or thirty of us a chance to find a place more hospitable than this island. This island looks like it could be just the peak of a volcano. What we're looking at now may be all there is to see. Worse still, this island could explode on us."

I saw a few people nod appreciatively at his suggestion. I was surprised when he interrupted my talk, but actually shocked by his apparent willingness to sail away and desert any of us, people who have lived and worked together so long. I needed to respond and get everyone back on track. I also recognized that Gunnar's real goal might have been to assert himself as our new leader. That would be all right with me, but right now the important thing is getting us to work together to achieve safety.

"Thanks Gunnar. That's an interesting suggestion, and we might want to think about rebuilding those rafts for the future. But I can't even conceive of a plan that might mean abandoning some of us while others sail off to safety. I know that's not what you meant Gunnar, but right now we are so few and have lost so many of our friends from Serenity Cove, that whatever we do has to be in the best interest of everyone's safety and survival."

Deadly silence followed. That was not a statement I had intended to make, but it was an emotion and I knew must control all of my future thoughts and actions until the day we were all safe and secure once again. Finally, I broke the silence and resumed the talk I had planned.

"It's definitely worthwhile to see if any of the rafts can be made usable again, but for now the fastest way to discover whether or not there is any possible future for us on this island is to find a way through or around those cliffs we're looking at. This will require a lot of climbing. I'm ready to go, but, as I said earlier, I can't go alone. Nobody should attempt a climb like that alone. I need one or two people willing to explore with me. I'm looking for volunteers."

"While we're gone, some of the rest of you can continue what you were doing and see if you can put some of the rafts back together. If you can reassemble them, secure them as far away from the water as possible in case the tide rises over the next few hours. Right now, I'm hoping to find a couple of volunteers to come climbing with me?"

I anticipated lots of volunteers and an immediate response. When that didn't happen right away I realized Gunnar's proposal had created doubts. I watched as heads turned, as our young men and women assessed the imposing cliffs that made up our Northern horizon. Lots of heads were shaking dispiritedly from side to side. A few were trying to avoid catching my eye. Finally, I could see a few hands waving enthusiastically. Joe Westfall's hand came up first, followed quickly by two more as the Abrams twins both volunteered. My sister Zoey let go of a rope she was using to tighten the canvas. Her hand shot up. I thought about each of them before speaking.

"This will be a dangerous venture. You all know that as well as I do. For that reason, I don't think I have any right to ask two people from the same family. Zoey, that lets you out. My thanks as always for your support." Zoey is always ready to argue with me, ever since we were very little kids, so I wasn't surprised when she objected to my consigning her to "woman's work."

"Carl Johnson, you know I am just as capable of leading that expedition as you are! Why don't you stay here and sew the sails with Nancy, while I lead the exploration?"

"Zoey, this isn't the time for this. I know how capable you are, but I think this is my job. It would have been Dad's job if he wasn't so exhausted. Now please let me get on with finding people who will join me on the climb?"

"Yeah, sure, go ahead. I just didn't want you to think you have to be in charge of everything. You're not Dad." A few of the younger kids were nudging one another, distracted and entertained by our squabbling.

I looked over to where the Abrams twins were standing, both with their arms raised high. "Jack and Sandy, I will be happy to have either one of you with me, but not both. Why don't you decide between you. Whatever you decide will be fine with me." I turned to Joe Westfall. I knew Joe well. He was my son Steven's best friend. He's a good kid and a strong athlete, but only seventeen. "Joe, I would love to have you, but I want you to check with your parents first. You're too young to make this decision without their agreement. Please, guys, decide right away. I think we need to get started as soon as possible."

I watched as Joe went over to wake up his parents and to get permission to come. I knew Joe would be an asset. He's big and strong and a great athlete. He was always best at every sport while our kids were growing up. His parents, Sam and Sarah Westfall are old timers. They had been on Getaway Island long before our family first arrived. The Westfalls are among our closest family friends. Each of us has a real relationship with a member of their family. Joe is their pride and joy. Their other son, Richie, is my daughter Emily's boyfriend. He is very bright, rather intellectual, always into books. I expected Joe to come running over with a Yes, but I guess I underestimated his mother Sarah's concern for her seventeen-year-old. I heard him pleading with her. She finally gave in and he came running to give me the good news. I was surprised to see that Sandy Abrams rather than her twin brother Jake was to be the third member of our crew. She had a big smile on her face.

"We both wanted to go. We bucked up and I won. "

My wife Nancy was furious with me. "Why would you start a meeting like that and spring it on everyone without even discussing it with me? You could have left it to the younger guys. Emily was crying after that meeting worrying about you. She's afraid you'll get lost and won't come back. Now Stevie wants to go with you. I won't allow it."

"Honey, the climb will take hours, and there may be places where decisions have to be made to go on or turn back. Do you think we should leave decisions like that entirely to our teenagers?"

"I know, but why does it always have to be you? You're just like your father. You think you have to be in charge of everything." I could feel the tears running down her cheeks as we hugged.

"Honey, I'll be all right. I promise. I want you to keep checking on Mom and Dad. As soon as they wake up you'll be the one to brief them on what is happening." We broke apart as Sandy and Joe joined us. They had just said their goodbyes to their families and were raring to go.

"OK, kids. Let's go. The sooner we start the better."

We walked toward the East end of the beach. Our rafts, still very much in evidence, were on the West side. Everyone was following us and they looked as though they were planning to watch our progress for as long as they were able to keep us in sight. I had already figured out where we would begin our climb. There was no way we would be able to climb safely through that mess of jagged rocks on the side where we landed. It didn't take us long to get to the other end of the beach. That's where the four of us made our first stop to analyze and plan. The near landscape looked like a pile of enormous granite boulders standing between us and the actual cliff. At least the boulders weren't the pointed spear-like rocks like those we encountered when our rafts crashed on the other side.

I did a quick apparel check and was pleased to see we all had on good climbing sneakers. Our only other helpful climbing equipment was a coil of the nylon line that had formerly been part of the rigging of our small sailboats back on Getaway. I started to climb the nearest boulder, trying to pull my way up, but would never have made it to the top on my own without Joe pushing me up from behind. When I finally felt secure on top of that first boulder, I threw my rope down to Sandy. She grabbed the rope, but barely needed it. She practically ran up the boulder. If I was worried about bringing a girl along, I stopped worrying that minute. Joe also scrambled up without any real help from me. We heard applause and cheering from the beach as soon as Joe made it onto the top. The three of us sat together for a minute on the top of our first conquest. Then down we went over the other side. We had to be careful going down. If we went too quickly, we ran the risk of spraining or breaking an ankle when we hit the ground. There were still several more boulders ahead of us. We quickly established a pattern. Joe would scramble up first, throw me a rope. I would follow with Sandy bringing up the rear. The two of them were very diplomatic when they actually took the lead. I understood they were protecting me and I was very thankful they were with me. They were great kids and the three of us worked well together. We climbed up and over boulder after boulder until we finally reached a flat sandy spot just before the face of the actual cliff.

Now standing very close to the front of the cliff, it didn't look quite so impassable. We could see footholds and cracks, but even better, there seemed to be a narrow ledge spiraling upward. At some points the ledge appeared only a few inches wide, but at others it was broader and looked relatively safe, hard to tell from the ground. For real climbers it might be a breeze, but to me it appeared a formidable challenge. I suggested we should all be tied together for the rest of the climb, and they readily agreed. I think they agreed because they were worried about me. It was apparent to all of us; the two of them were in much better physical shape than me. Bowing to reality, and exercising common sense rather than bravado, I told Joe to take the lead. He started by leaping onto the low point of the ledge, and pulling the rope taut as I followed up. Sandy came right behind me and we started climbing, leaning hard against the side of the cliff, the rope hanging loosely on the outside. We climbed steadily for about half an hour and I was already gasping for breath.

"Hey, let's take a rest stop, guys."

"Sure, whatever you say, Carl." Joe wasn't even slightly winded. I really needed a break. We all leaned back against the cliff and looked back and down. Our ledge had taken us a long way from where we started and we were now about a hundred feet above beach level. From this distance we still clearly saw our families hard at work below. I looked for the spot where Dad and Mom had been sleeping, and they were no longer there. I scanned the beach and finally spotted Dad by the edge of the water directing traffic. It was good to see he was back in charge and I was thankful he wasn't actually in the water dragging things from the broken-up rafts. The tide was rising around the group working to rescue what they could, and I wondered how much longer they'd be able to work before the waves would make it impossible. They had been able to bring two rafts that were still intact onto the beach and had secured them, tethering them to one of the scrubby bushes that poked through the face of the cliff near our landing place.

When we started climbing we were heading westward

toward the sun, but now the widening ledge had us gradually turning a corner toward the North. Five minutes after we rested, we no longer saw the beach. As we continued around the bend, the land below us was an evergreen forest that stretched out for a mile or two. It promised shade from the blazing sun beating down on the beach. Beyond the forest there was a large clearing, and then finally more beach and, after that, the ocean. We kept walking along the ledge and it widened into a true path. We walked side by side as the path led us toward the forest below. We had a decision to make. We could now see what was below, and it looked like a promising place to settle. I wondered whether we needed to explore further or if we should just go back now and get everyone off the beach.

I decided it looked like a safe haven ahead. I called a halt. We had been climbing for at least two hours, and at this point, we knew what we came to find out. It was a fairly large island, good enough soil to support a forest and the promise of potential shelter.

Our families would to be worrying about us, "I think we should go back, get everyone together and plan to bring everyone with us as soon as possible."

Joe and Sandy listened politely, but I could see they really wanted to keep going. They were both excited by what they saw and were eager to see more. I understood how they felt and hesitated to ignore their feelings.

" It's very tempting to keep going down and see it first hand, but I think it is more important to get back as quickly as possible to tell everybody the island looks promising. Then we'll have a chance to get everybody moving as early as possible tomorrow." Sandy's bright smile disappeared. Her facial expressions went from enthusiastic to a bland neutral. She was obviously unhappy with what I was saying. "It won't take us that long to get down there. Who knows what might be hidden by all of those trees?!"

Joe was equally excited, but more cautious. "I think we should at least get down to ground level to make sure it's safe. I have a feeling that there are people down there, and that we're not alone on this island. I'm betting there are people down there."

"Is that just a feeling or have you seen something I don't see that makes you think there are people here?"

"There must be people. Take a look off in the distance to where you can see the ocean. Right before the edge of the water it looks like a huge clearing in the forest. Do you see what I mean? That doesn't look like a natural clearing. It looks carved out by people, people who knew what they were doing. It looks much too even .I can't see much detail from here, but I think I see cabins or at least tents, or some type of shelter."

"That's amazing, Joe! Your eyesight is obviously better than mine. I don't see anything that look like cabins or tents! Even if you're right, that still shouldn't make us want to delay getting everybody off that narrow beach. Is there something you're afraid of that you just don't want to say?"

"I know it's going to sound crazy, but what if they're wild people who have lived here for centuries, tribes who have never had contact with civilized people before? What if they're savages and decide they want to eat us for dinner?" Sandy laughed, as if he was being ridiculous. Joe's suggestion wasn't so outrageous to me. Still, I wanted to calm his fears.

"Anything is possible, but whatever is down there we really don't have a choice. We can't safely stay on that beach, we can't survive there. We've got to get ourselves settled someplace a whole lot safer. And from what I see everything ahead looks like an improvement."

We agreed to compromise by walking down for another half hour. Then we would reassess. We started walking again and details started to emerge. There were indeed signs of human activity below and none of it looked particularly threatening. We stopped to take in what appeared to be a managed forest, and what must have been an actual path system through the forest, all the way from the bottom of the cliff to the clearing before the ocean. We were all satisfied we had seen enough. It was time to turn back.

As we climbed back toward the beach and finally over the last of the boulders, we could see everyone gathered in a circle on the beach. They must have been watching our progress as we came down the ledge and over the huge boulders. They were waiting expectantly for our return, and our report, hoping for good news. Spread out in front of them were bags of sandwiches and bottled drinks rescued from the rafts. Wow! My stomach was starting to growl. Until I looked down I didn't realize how hungry I was. This would be our first real attempt at a meal since we left Getaway Island. It looked as though every bit of food that was saved from the rafts was there, spread out on the beach. In addition to the sandwiches, I saw a few pieces of fruit, dried and bagged for munching on the trail and even a few of our homemade Getaway Candy bars. It was all there, the lunches and snacks that had been intended to last us only an hour or so from home until we reached the mainland. Family groups were gathered together. My family clustered around Mom and Dad. Zoey and Hank and their kids were on one side. Nancy, Steve and Emily on the other.

They had all been watching and waiting so it wasn't surprising they let out a whoop and came running toward us. As soon as I slid down onto the beach from the last of the boulders, I was surrounded. Stevie and Emily were hugging me and Nancy was just behind, tears rolling down her cheeks as relief came from what must have been anxious hours for all of them. I saw the Westfalls surrounding Joe, and the whole Abrams clan practically smothered Sandy. After lots of hugs and kisses, I knew it was time to answer questions. I headed to where Mom, Dad, Zoey, Hank and my niece and nephew were waiting. Then there were more hugs, kisses and exclamations of relief.

After all of the excited greetings, I briefed Mom and Dad on our adventure. Joe and Sandy were undoubtedly telling their families stories similar to mine. It didn't take long before everyone came over, circling our family, waiting for Dad to call a meeting. I had to admire him. He must be close to seventy now, but it seemed clear that he still commanded the group.

Every one of us sat quietly, respectfully listening as he outlined what he thought we should do. After going over everything, tasks were assigned. We would plan to move first thing in the morning. We got ourselves and our things ready to go before total darkness settled in.

There are forty-six of us including eight young children. I often wondered if any of the others managed to make it to any other land, and were still alive somewhere. We'd all been so busy just trying to survive that we hadn't had time to mourn properly or even to speculate what might have happened to the others. I prayed that some of them made it. Whether they did or didn't, I knew we would never see any of them again. I allowed myself a few minutes to ruminate and then it was time to get back to work.

Mal Abrams, Sam Westfall and Hank were in charge of determining what we needed and what we hoped to be able to carry with us. Everything that had been salvaged was laid out up against the rocks at the back of the beach. It wasn't my job, but I couldn't keep myself from putting in my two cents. Joe, Sandy and I were the ones who knew what we would need just to make the climb without losing anybody.

"Hi, guys. Do you need any help?" Hank looked at me as though I was crazy.

"Carl, go get some sleep. You guys had a long hard day, and we'll count on you leading the way tomorrow. We'll take care of this. It's easy enough to figure out what we'll need. The big issue will be trying to determine how much we can carry. We watched as you guys climbed over those boulders. The three of you may have been alone, but as long as you were in sight everybody here was watching you. We have a pretty good idea of how tough the going will be." Mal and Sam were nodding their heads in agreement.

"Listen to your brother-in-law. Get some rest now. You can check our decisions in the morning before we go."

"Okay, I get it! I'm out of here." My family was sharing a tent with Zoey and Hank and their kids. I found everyone wide awake and so nervous and excited about the following day's trip that they couldn't begin to get ready for sleep. Nancy had tried to calm our kids, but without much success. Eventually they quieted down. Even Nancy fell asleep. But I was too wired, and Zoey wasn't about to go to sleep until Hank came back. I think Zoey was still a little upset that she hadn't had a more important role to play. I got to go climbing today, Hank was on the planning committee and she just stayed here with the kids. Growing up she was clearly the athlete in the family. Well, she'll have her chance tomorrow.

Characters in the Novel, Part 2

Jethro & Sarah Smith Family & Son Elijah (19)

Horace Smith (Jethro's brother)

Isaiah & Leah Smith Family & Twins Sammy & Ruth

James & Sonia Hanson Family & Daughter Olivia (19)

Chapter 7

The Believers

"Daddy, are you home? Daddy, this is important! Sammy and I saw strangers, new people who don't live here!"

Isaiah came into the room. "Are you two making up a story? Are you playing a game or just trying to fool your father?

"They were on the path just above the great forest. Who do you think they are? Where did they come from? Are they invaders?"

"Nobody has ever come down that path. It's not possible."

"It's true, Daddy, we're not making it up! I know it's impossible, but they were really there. We were picking berries, and we looked up and there they were. It was two men and a woman. They looked very big and strong. The two men were enormous, but even the woman was bigger than anybody here, even bigger than Horace. I bet they were from another planet. They couldn't be normal humans. We watched them a long time as they were walking. They were coming down and down and down, and suddenly they stopped to talk. They were pretty close to where we were then. We just held our breath while we watched them. We didn't know what they would do if they saw us. We crawled under the bushes to get closer. We heard their voices but we couldn't hear what they were saying. They sounded like the people from some other country, not

America. After talking for a few minutes, they just turned around and started back up the trail. Once they started the other way, Ruth and I ran all the way home to warn everybody."

"Good thinking! We have to tell Jethro right now. Both of you come with me. I want you to tell him exactly what you saw. I was sure this would happen sooner or later. People were bound to come and rescue us, but I thought they would come from the sea, not the land. We don't know who these people are or what their intentions may be. Let's hope they will be friends and not enemies. Jethro will know what to do. Maybe he'll call an emergency defense meeting. "

"Can we come to the defense meeting? You wouldn't let us come to the last one. You said we were too young."

"You were too young then, but you're not too young now. Let's get over to Jethro's house."

Jethro didn't interrupt as they repeated what they had told their father. He could see how animated the twins were, and more important how very agitated Isaiah was. "Ok, tell me again, but this time only one of you. Ruth, you tell me."

"It was just like we said before. We were picking berries at the edge of the big forest when we heard voices, looked up, and saw these three gigantic people coming down the path. We couldn't hear what they were saying, but whatever it was, when they finished talking and drinking water from small bottles, they turned around and started back up the path, and we ran back to tell Daddy."

"Isaiah, do these two ever make up stories?"

"Neither one of them would ever make up a story like this. You know that. I told you years ago we were bound to be found eventually. The world is getting more and more crowded. Sooner or later every little island in the world will be populated. These may be people driven by overcrowding who have come to see about starting a new settlement on this island, small as it is. Best of all would be if the Lord has answered our prayers and they are here to rescue us."

"Isaiah, we've all heard your theories before, but this isn't a time to speculate on the future. Right now, we have a situation to deal with, not sooner or later. We need to determine pretty quickly is if this is a threat or if God has finally decided to smile upon us with most wonderful good fortune... or it may be something else."

Jethro turned to his brother. "Horace, you've been very quiet. That's not like you. what do you think?"

"I think it's time to oil up our rifles and shot guns, and form a proper welcoming committee for them. They're invading our island."

"Why are you always so damn belligerent? Why would you 'welcome' them as invaders? They may well be our rescuers. They have to have come by boat, and the boat that brought them could be our lifeline to the old world. They could have come from anywhere and for any reason or for no reason at all! Maybe they're adventurers or from an amateur climbing club that spotted our island as a challenge. We can't know who they are or what they want until we meet them. I like to think the Lord is providing these people as our ticket off this island and back to the world our great great grandparents left years ago."

Horace couldn't help interrupting his big brother. "Jethro, you may be our official leader and you are often right, but you are not always right. You should listen to me. You appointed me Head of Defense years ago, and this may just be the occasion you appointed me to take care of. The way I see it, they could be anyone and come from anywhere, but WHY did they come? I doubt they were sent by the Lord to deliver us from this accursed island. If their intentions are honorable why would they dock their boat on the other side of the mountain? We've always assumed there is no place to land a boat on the other side. We've also assumed that there is no way around the mountain from the other side. On the other hand, if Isaiah's children are telling the truth, those old assumptions appear to be false. People have come from that side and we never thought of having to defend ourselves from that side. Why would they approach us from the mountain rather than the sea? The only reason I can think for them to dock on the other side is to surprise us and take over the island."

Jethro shook his head." Horace, you always have a way of looking on the dark side of things. How did you ever concoct such a theory? Nobody in the world even knows we're here. Somehow, they got here, probably by accident; although I do agree that we can't assume they are peaceful. I remember stories our parents told us about the days before the epidemic. They said there were constant wars and there was lawlessness everywhere. Our ancestors may have run away from the Great Epidemic, but there were all kinds of other problems. These people the kids saw could be here to take over the island, or maybe they're refugees too or they may simply have stumbled on the island, and don't even know we exist. I think the best thing we can do is greet them with flowers and fruit and welcome them as friends. If we're friendly, they are most likely to respond in kind."

Isaiah, who had been listening to the brothers arguing, as they frequently did, spoke up as a potential voice of reason. "Jethro, you're right, Horace often looks on the dark side. He could also be right in this case, and I think we can't afford to be unprepared. We can be welcoming and friendly, but I think we have to appear with a show of force as well so they know we can protect ourselves if necessary. It wouldn't hurt to greet them peacefully, but with a few of our men carrying rifles on their shoulders."

"Jethro, the three of us can't make this decision alone. I suggest you call a town meeting right now."

"I'll ring the bell and tell the rest what's happening. Then we can start getting ready." Jethro turned to his wife, who was uncharacteristically quiet. "Sarah, what do you think?"

"I think you and Isaiah are both right. Those people who were on the path are bound to return and they will come with additional people. A few of us, not too many, should meet them at the bottom of the path, as a welcoming committee. We should have garlands of flowers around our neck as a symbol of peaceful intentions, and if we come bearing platters of food that will surely send a message of friendliness. I can't see any need to show weapons, but it might be prudent to have a few of our best riflemen ready and out of sight in the woods nearby, just in case.... If the newcomers appear friendly, there is no need for them ever to see that we also were prepared to defend ourselves."

Chapter 8
Carl

A New Beginning

As we started on the downhill side of the ledge, the kids were suddenly reenergized. They had dragged and grumbled during the perilous long uphill climb, but now they were suddenly running ahead. The eight of them had rounded a bend in the path and were out of sight. I think we had actually slowed down some because we were worried about our parents' aches and pains since early in our climb. We had to push and pull them up and over those enormous boulders before we got to the actual ledge. Mom had a terrible time and I could see how she hated having to be helped over by two or more young people.

I was speculating on what might lie ahead, when I heard excited screaming, and saw the kids running back toward us. Zoey's daughter Janice was the first to get to us, panting and red in the face. "There are people down there! We saw them, people waiting at the bottom of the path. Three or four of them are waiting there holding big platters loaded with what looked like food. I'm sure it was food. and there were baskets sitting near them on the ground that were also filled with food. "

"Can we run down and get some, or do we have to wait for

you?" That was Janice's brother Mark. No matter what the situation, food always came first with him. By now our long line had telescoped, and almost everyone could hear most of Janice's news. I shouted back so Mom and Dad, the Senior Westfalls and Mal and Jill Abrams, who were at the very back would hear the news as well. It certainly sounded good to me.

I shouted to him. "Dad, what do you think?"

He shouted back to me. "Full speed ahead. People waiting with food sounds very civilized to me."

Everyone cheered, and I had to restrain the kids who wanted to charge ahead. "No running ahead now. Wait for us." A few minutes later, we were on level ground at the bottom and it was just as Janice said. Four rather small people were waiting there. It was difficult to determine their racial or national origin from their skin color which seemed a combination of white, brown, red and yellow. There was no question they were offering us platters of mouth-watering looking slices of watermelon, peaches, plums and a fruit I could not identify. We all waited as Mom and Dad moved to the front and took the lead. As Dad approached the strangers waiting below he spread his arms wide, with open hands facing skyward to show we come in peace. To me, he looked worn out, but tired as he was, his eyes were bright and his whole demeanor was beaming happiness.

He spoke very slowly, assuming they might speak a different language and hoping if he spoke slowly enough he might be understood.

"We come in peace."

A very small dark-skinned woman greeted us. She spoke excitedly and with a typically northern New England twang. "Welcome! Welcome! Welcome strangers! My name is Sarah, and we are all so happy to see you. We also speak English. Our people came to this island from America a very long time ago. We have been waiting for years for someone from America to find us and to carry us back home with them. And now here you are. Your appearance proves that The Lord can still produce miracles."

A rather short man with dark leathery skin and a neatly trimmed beard stepped forward. He also had a broad smile on his face. "Welcome! I join my wife Sarah in bidding you welcome. My name is Jethro. I am Chairman of our fellowship here on Forever Island. We are all so happy to see you." He extended his hand toward Dad and the two of them shook hands warmly. "We invite your family to join us in the shade of our great forest where we have tables with some light refreshment and drinks ready for you. You must all be hot and tired after climbing up and around that mountain."

He was right about that. We were all hot and tired and a few of us were at the edge of exhaustion. Mom was limping slightly and I could see Jill Abrams leaning heavily against her son Jack. He was just about carrying her down the last little ridge until she had both feet firmly on flat ground. Sam and Marge Westfall were moving very slowly, leaning heavily against one another for support.

Our hosts, Jethro and Sarah, beckoned us to follow them into a shaded area below, where we were greeted by about half a dozen other small adults and a number of little children, jumping about excitedly. Makeshift tables awaited us, laden with platters, some with a rich assortment of fruit, others with a variety of sandwiches. There were also pitchers of juice and some with delicious cold clear water. We were so hungry and thirsty we showed little restraint in attacking the feast we saw before us. We never envisioned such a welcome when we landed on this seemingly harsh island two days before. It looked to me as though we had just arrived at our very own land of milk and honey. I know that nothing is ever really perfect, but it was clear these people had gone out of their way to be as welcoming as possible. It seemed like we had fallen into some really good luck! I knew it was premature to assume all would be well, but I was optimistic. From the time we first stepped down into their world, our hosts were extraordinarily gracious, treating us as honored guests.

When it became obvious we were sated, having gorged ourselves with their delicious fruit and generous sandwiches, their leader Jethro came over to talk with Dad. Since I was still concerned about both Mom and Dad after the strenuous climb, it seemed important to stand by Dad and listen as the two men spoke together.

"It appears you have enjoyed the little luncheon we prepared for you, and your people must be exhausted after your long climb around the mountain. Why don't we let everyone rest while I tell you who we are. And you can also tell us your story. We are part of a fellowship of a much larger group, people of true faith called Believers. Among our beliefs is the welcoming of strangers and extending our hospitality to them in their new surroundings. We'll do our best to fulfill that obligation.

"Please let your people know that we have a rather long walk ahead of us through the great forest to our village and they should take this opportunity to rest. I'm sorry I cannot offer other means of transport for all of you. However, we do have a few pony carts, which delivered the food you have just enjoyed. The carts can be made available for any of your people who will need assistance after your difficult climb."

"Thank you on behalf of our whole group for this absolutely wonderful meal. We feel refreshed and revived and I think we can to proceed without a formal rest period. And, I thank you for offering the possibility of rides for those who need them. I'll check with my wife Rachel, and some of the other older members of our group to see if they could use a ride. Speaking for myself, the prospect of a good walk on flat ground sounds very appealing. It seems you are inviting us to your village? Your kindness to strangers is much appreciated. We won't require luxurious housing, but a few nights with a roof over our heads would be great."

"Yes, of course, your people must stay with us while we all make our plans. To be perfectly frank with you, your arrival has given us all great optimism. After you have had a chance to rest up in our village, we hope to be able to join with you on your ship and travel with you to some civilized place in the world. We have been awaiting your arrival for a very long time. Our people have been here for more than seventy years and some were beginning to lose faith that our rescue would ever come. I cannot wait to learn how you heard about us, and our island."

I was about to interrupt and disabuse him of the notion that we had a ship, when Dad turned toward me and put his forefinger across his lips in the universal symbol for silence. I wasn't sure what his reasons were. However, if he thought it best not to divulge our current desperate circumstances until we get to know these people who called themselves Believers, I agreed. I kept my mouth shut and listened as Dad continued.

"We look forward to visiting with you in your village and getting acquainted with all you have accomplished here. After we've been here a day or two, we can start to discuss plans for the future."

Jethro, Sarah and two other local men led us from the picnic area into their glorious forest. It was comfortably cool in the forest, which was primarily Pines and Hemlocks, with a scattering of a few trees which looked suspiciously like our own magical White Bark Spruce trees. I wasn't the only one who noticed them. Gunnar called out "Wow! They have White Bark Spruce trees here. I didn't think they grew anyplace other than Getaway Island."

Dad called back loud enough for all of us to hear." Yes, they're White Bark Spruce for sure. Great to see old friends on a new island."

Through the trees I also saw a large flock of sheep grazing, apparently on their own. Small birds darted across our path and between trees. This forest was a delight, divided neatly by the path we were on, which ran through the middle, straight as an arrow from the bottom of the mountain all the way to a clearing about three quarters of a mile ahead. The path itself had been carefully constructed with hard packed clay. There were several narrow lanes on either side of the path that seemed to disappear into the depths of the trees. The entire forest appeared remarkably clear of debris and fallen limbs.

As we came within a few hundred yards of what appeared to be the Village center, Jethro was met by a man he introduced as Isaiah. Isaiah, it seemed, would be our guide to show us around town. Jethro explained that he would be busy arranging for temporary housing for all of us. Before he left us, he asked how many there were of us. I came up with the number forty-eight. With that information, he started down what he referred to as Center Street. Our new guide, Isaiah, was accompanied by his children Ruth and Sammy, who we had already met at the bottom of the mountain. Ruth proudly told us she and her brother were the first to see us, having spotted us the day before when Joe, Sandy, and I had come came down on our exploratory venture. They had been out picking berries in the area. "We were scared when we saw you. You are all so big compared to us. We ran back to tell Mommy and Daddy. Daddy took us with him to tell Jethro. Jethro didn't believe us at first, but Daddy told him we don't make up stories, and we don't!"

"So that is how you all knew we were coming and prepared such a special welcome for us when we came down the mountain. Thank you for telling your parents."

We finally arrived at the large open area. I saw a real town spread out ahead of us. There were rows of cabins, which look well-made and solid, a lot like our cabins in Serenity Cove. As we entered the large open area, it was clear that this was the primary gathering place for the town. There was a rambling wooden structure just to our right that looked like a meeting hall, and on our left was a small wooden grandstand, like one you would expect to find on a high school football field. Straight ahead, on the far side of the open space, I saw streets, each with rows of houses. My eyes automatically scanned the streets where the people lived, trying to estimate the size of the community. It helped that the streets appeared to be laid out in a grid pattern, going to the left and right of Center Street. On the first couple of streets there looked to be are ten cabins per street, five on each side of Center Street. From front to back there were a total of five cross streets. I assumed the same number of cabins were on each street, making a total of fifty cabins. If there was an average of four people to a cabin, the total population would be about two hundred people.

There were quite a few people out in the town square, obviously intending to get a glimpse of us first hand. Most of them were going about normal activities, but some surreptitiously glanced our way. Some looked worried as we passed close to them. A few smiled and started clapping as we passed by, as though we were performers newly arrived for their entertainment. They are almost uniformly short, about a head shorter than most Americans. They appeared healthy, well fed, and carefully dressed. I saw children playing. It was hard to tell the young boys from the girls as all had their hair cut close to their scalps. I wonder if that is protection against bugs or simply their traditional hair style.

How could they accommodate us if all of those cabins have people living in them? I decided to stop speculating and just ask. "Isaiah, has your community had any guests before ?"

Isaiah laughed, "People don't just drop in here. To the best of my knowledge there have been no visitors ever until your arrival."

"How you can possibly house so many of us as guests? I'm assuming that all of the cabins have current occupants."

"Yes, the cabins are all filled with our people, but don't be concerned. Jethro will figure out something. He and I don't always see eye to eye, but there is nobody in the world who could possibly be a better organizer than Jethro. He and his brother are masters. You'll see, they'll figure out something that works. He asked me to show you around to give himself time to come up with that solution. There isn't really that much for me to show here in town. We do have some interesting fruit trees and other farm areas in part of the forest, but there's time for that when you and your people are not so tired. I'll just take you for a walk down Center Street to the port. There are benches there and nice shade trees where you can all relax and watch our fishermen at work until Jethro has worked out a plan to house all of you. I'm sure you'll meet his brother Horace with him when he comes to take over from me. Horace is not as easy to get along with as Jethro, but he is a master builder. He's often the one who makes Jethro's plans happen."

When Jethro rejoined us he was accompanied by his much larger brother Horace, who spoke gruffly and didn't seem nearly as happy to see us as Jethro and Isaiah or any of the others we had met when we first arrived. However, he seemed pleasant 'enough' as he escorted all of us to our tents, and showed us how to open and close the flaps. Then he took us to an enormous stack of sleeping mats for our entire group, making sure to allocate the proper number for each family. I can't imagine why they would have such a large supply of mats available, but they did. For that matter, how and why did they happen to have five huge tents? These people were a puzzle, as I supposed we were to them.

Before he showed us to our tents, Jethro had given us the choice of being split up and housed in the homes of a large number of their families who had volunteered to take us in. Dad put it to an immediate vote and overwhelmingly the sentiment was clear that we wanted to keep family groups together; that nobody wanted to be separated so soon after our arrival at what may well be our new home for the indefinite future. We were happy to be sheltered in tents for the time being. When Dad relayed our response to Jethro, Horace, and Isaiah, he made sure to emphasize how much we appreciated the offer made by people who don't even know us. Dad said he understood we might be more comfortable in their homes, but would prefer to keep our families together. Jethro and Isaiah both said they understood how we felt. Horace reiterated instructions to all of us on how to use the tents. Then he led one member of each family to an area where several outhouses were located in the forest a reasonable distance from the tents.

We had a family meeting that night. Our whole family gathered in our tent; one of five very large tents Jethro's brother had erected for us. They were set at the edge of the town center, backed against the forest, partially shielding them from the harsh daytime sun.

There we were having our first official family meeting in our new world. All of our families were doing the same in their tents. Before he left us to get settled, Jethro addressed a question to us all, "Would you be ready and willing to attend a community wide meeting as soon as tomorrow, for our two communities to get to know one another, and so that we can discuss evacuation plans for our people?"

Jethro's seemingly imperturbable calm deserted him as he continued beyond the simple question he had asked.

"You must forgive me if I seem forward with this request for a meeting so soon after your arrival, but it may not be obvious to you who have lived your lives in freedom how eager we are to rejoin the rest of the world. Though this is our home and we are certainly used to it, those of us who live here now have felt ourselves stranded here all of our lives, cut off from the rest of the world. Our parents were marooned here on this island for most of their lives, though a few of them told stories of what life was like before they came to this island. Our grandparents and great grandparents, who left their homes seeking freedom from persecution and a quest for a better life, boarded a ship more than seventy years ago . Their ship went down in a terrible storm just off the coast of this island and they felt blessed to reach this shore, where they spent the last years of their lives. They achieved their goal. There was nobody here to persecute them, but they never dreamed there would be no escape from this island. It may be difficult for you to understand the sense of loss and isolation this separation from the world has built in all of us. So, we do look forward to a meeting to welcome you for your short stay with us, but most important, to hear of your plans for our rescue."

The request for us to attend a meeting the next morning was addressed to all of us, but it was clear Dad would be the one to respond. Before he responded, I could see Dad absorbing the information, as well as Jethro's emotion. After a moment of reflection, he looked over at the other senior members of our community. Gunnar Svenson, Harry Pollard, Sam Westfall and Sally Brownstein. Each of them gave an affirmative nod. That was all Dad needed.

"Yes, Jethro. We will look forward to a pleasant meeting and discussion with your generously welcoming clan tomorrow."

When we got to a meeting in our own family tent, we all expressed the sense that the islanders appear to be delightful people, and they certainly had been wonderful to us so far. We knew they were understandingly laboring under the mistaken impression that we had a ship anchored on the other side of the mountain and that we will would take them all with us when we were to leave. We knew it would come as a shock and a blow to them when they learned the truth; that there is no ship; that there is no evacuation plan; that we considered ourselves lucky to have survived after our harrowing adventure with the tides and winds just two days ago and that we have not had much chance to think beyond our own survival. I wondered what their reaction would be toward us when they learned that we weren't going to be their saviors. We speculated a bit about our hosts and about what the future was likely to bring for us, but we were too tired to talk for long. Even our kids, who are usually bubbling with energy long after their parents were ready for bed, even they were ready for sleep.

Chapter 9
Carl

Haven or Home

The next day, we met with Jethro and the entire Believers community. As we entered the meeting house I could see it was filled with the islanders. Directly opposite the entrance door, on the far wall, there was a small stage. To our left the room was packed by residents, seated in rows facing us like an audience, with our people the presumed performers. We were escorted to tables, arranged by family groups, and laden with a luxurious array of breakfast foods.

Isaiah was standing on the stage. Seated behind him was his wife Leah, one of the lovely diminutive women who had first greeted us when we reached the bottom of the mountain. Seated beside her were their children, Sammy and Ruth. Jethro, his wife Sarah, and their son Elijah were also seated on the stage, but judging from the seating arrangement, it was Isaiah who was about to chair the meeting. Isaiah held a large cardboard megaphone like those I remember from way back when I was a boy and was entered in community races. He faced us and directed his words toward us.

"Dear new friends, I hope you all had a good night's sleep. I know you were all very tired after your strenuous day. As tired as you were last night, I am sure you are also very hungry this morning. I urge you to enjoy your breakfast. Do not hesitate. I will not be insulted that you eat while I speak. We have had our breakfast in our own homes earlier this morning. We are happy to welcome you, and think you might wish to know who we are, and the circumstances which have us living here. We also want to learn more about and you and the community from which you have recently sailed. Of course, everyone here is anxious to hear about how you plan to help those of us who wish to leave the island and resettle in an established country which is willing to accept our people. I must tell you from the start, I believe our entire community will wish to be resettled in another land."

"Now for our history; I know from the few conversations we have had that your group all originally came from America. So, you may well be familiar with the name Believers. That is the generic title of our people. We call our specific Fellowship Believers, and that is what we are. We believe in All-mighty God, in righteous living, and in living a life of simplicity, devoid of the modern so-called improvements imposed upon the current world in the guise of progress."

"You may think of the Believers as one, but like most religions, there are several different branches, each of which identify as Believers Fellowships. Our branch is one of several Believer Fellowships. Originally, the Believers in America were all members of a more ancient Christian Fellowship which started in Switzerland. Once in America, the Believers settled in rural sections of Vermont and New Hampshire. Historically, we Believers have been clannish people, organizing ourselves into groups of twenty or so families, who live a simple life together from generation to generation. We are a very tolerant and openminded people, knowing that we, ourselves, have not always been accepted. Because of the history of our particular Fellowship, our members are racially quite different from the traditional Believers who came from Switzerland. We are smaller in stature and we have a somewhat different skin color. History has played a dominant role in who we are today."

"After the period known in your history books as the French-Indian Wars in the mid seventeen hundreds, there was much confusion among the several Native American tribes which had been involved. Several such tribes had internal disputes and broke apart. One such tribe called itself the Huchon People. The Huchons became nomadic for a time, wandering, looking for their own new homeland. They eventually settled in a largely unpopulated area of central New Hampshire."

"During that same time there were also several Believer Fellowships in northern New England. We were one of those. Our descendants settled in central New Hampshire, immediately adjacent to the territory claimed by the Huchons. Our Believer Fellowship and Huchon tribesmen lived side by side for a time with little contact between them. Ultimately, they began to mingle. And over a long period of time the mingling led to close social contact, and slowly the two became a new combined Fellowship. We are the descendants of those people. It is clear from our physical characteristics the Huchon genes prevailed physically, but in the realm of ideas we Believers were the winners. The Huchons adopted our faith and made it their own. They became Believers. We are those Believers several generations later."

"Because of our history, we in our Fellowship have not always been entirely at peace with ourselves, but we always try to live our lives according to the original tenets of the Believers Fellowships. Unfortunately, the older more traditional Believer Fellowships rejected us right from the start. They besmirched our reputation, calling us a mongrel race. They harassed us, forcing us to move further and further away from the main American homeland in rural New Hampshire. No matter how far we moved, it was never far enough to please them. Our fellowship has been discriminated against in every possible way. Eventually the discrimination produced such unhappiness and ill feeling in our people that our great grandparents resolved to leave New Hampshire and start a new community elsewhere."

"They carefully studied possible locations for the clan to relocate. They thought first to move to a sparsely settled western state. Then somebody convinced the elders of the time that the better move would be across the seas to the country called Greenland, which is very sparsely settled. Our people contracted with a highly reputable shipping company to provide a fine sailing vessel and a professional crew to transport the entire fellowship to Greenland. That decision created another crisis. Leaders of neighboring Fellowships pointed their fingers at us. How, they asked, can you choose to board a ship powered by an internal combustion machine, when we all reject such modern contrivances in our everyday life here on land? We had already had that debate internally and decided to continue with our decision. The alternate would be to go off on a sailing ship and on such a long journey, having to depend on wind currents alone simply did not make sense, particularly when there was now a much safer means of traveling over the ocean."

"Our people started their voyage in high good spirits, eager to get on with the next phase of our Fellowship life. On the third day at sea, tragedy struck as a huge storm hit, and the ship was blown off course, and ultimately went down. It must have been a hurricane. We were told by our grandparents who survived that they were tossed about for more than twenty-six hours, with the ship taking on water faster than it could be bailed out. Finally, the ship capsized just off shore, not a great distance from our current fishing piers."

"Many of our people drowned, including several members of the crew. Fortunately, a large number of our folks survived, as did some members of the ship's crew. However, too many died, including children of several who survived. We remember them all with an annual day of mourning in the fall of every year. The surviving crew members and their descendants are now also a part of our fellowship."

"Our people salvaged what they could from the ship. The ship was still intact and lying on its side not very far beneath the sea. Over many months, our ancestors were able to strip much of the wood from the hold of the ship before it became too water-logged to be useful and they brought it on shore. The hold of the ship had been filled with material for our new village in Greenland. Our people were able to salvage enough lumber to build all of the cabins you have seen, as well as this meeting hall, a warehouse which you will see not far from the port, and our very important fishing piers. They were also able to save all of the hand tools and the farming implements they had brought along with them for their new community. The Believers have always been farmers, and our grandparents and parents accepted the challenge, and made this land sufficiently productive to provide food for several generations. We have fruit trees laden with fruit and highly productive vegetable gardens. The waters just off shore provide an abundance of fish, and our forest is blessed with numerous small mammals, which makes it possible for us to occasionally even have meat as part of our diet. Our food supply lacks only the dairy products we would have had if they been able to save the three cows on board, none of which survived."

"We are now the third and fourth generations living on this island, on this land of plenty, but still dreaming about rescue and the regeneration of our society. Though we now think of this as our Land of Plenty for which we thank the Almighty, the reality is that food is plentiful in the warm months from late Spring until late Fall. By late Fall and early Winter, that ceases to be true. Our winters are cold enough so that we are able to store certain foods and make it through until Spring. In years with poor crops, it is a struggle all year long."

"We also need to finally escape from this island for the sake of our children and future generations. From the time our ancestors were stranded here they have made it a point to educate their children on our history and all other important areas of learning. Each succeeding generation has kept up that tradition. Our children are educated and are completely free here, but they deserve the opportunity that wider horizons would give them. In short, we long to rejoin the world, fully understanding all of the possible perils. That is our history, and that is our need. Now we look forward to hearing your history and hope to hear that you can accommodate a large number of additional passengers on your ship."

I was flattered to have been unanimously elected as spokesperson for our Getaway Island survivors. I stood facing the Believers for a moment without speaking. Isaiah handed the cardboard megaphone to me. I didn't think I would be able to hold that huge megaphone up to my mouth and see my audience. I would have no idea what anyone's reaction would be to what I was saying. I thanked him and set it down on the table. It was not an enviable task to be the one to break the news that we have no ship, and that we were survivors, not rescuers. We were immigrants on their island and likely to become their long-term neighbors.

"Thank you Isaiah, and thank you too Jethro, Sarah, Leah and all of you, all the members of your Fellowship. You have been extraordinary hosts. I wish we had it in our power to answer your hopes for deliverance from this island. You've assumed that we came by ship. We did not! We have no ship! I'm so sorry." I heard a gasp and saw a look of shock and puzzlement on nearby faces. I paused for a long moment, letting my news sink in. I felt..., but I there was no choice. I had to tell them. I wanted them to know right from the start who we were and where we come from, and to assure them we meant no harm and posed no threat.

"We arrived on your island just the day before yesterday on five crude homemade rafts. We were on those rafts because we had to escape the island where we've lived happily for decades. The sea level had been rising fast and has by now completely inundated our island. If we stayed we would have drowned."

"There were several populated communities on our island. We weren't the only ones. Tragically, most of the people in the other communities were unable to escape, and died under the sea. As we pulled away from shore on our rafts, we barely had time to understand the others were most likely gone, and we'll never know their fate for certain. Nor have we had time to properly mourn their loss. Our small group, knowing that the water level was rising steadily, had made plans for our escape some time in advance of the actual crisis. We cut down trees and built rafts. We secured the rafts on the beachhead from which we would have to depart if and when the tides reached the critical level. That day came, and our rafts were right where we needed them. Once we embarked, the storm tides grabbed us, spun us around, tossing us back and forth. We were completely powerless. We paddled for hours and that's probably what kept us upright, but we went wherever the wind and water took us. We kept looking and hoping to find land. When we spotted this island after hours of being tossed about, we could tell the current seemed to be pushing us toward this island. The seas were still very rough as we approached and our rafts smashed against the huge boulders which border the very narrow beach on the other side of this island. Because there was no possibility of long-term safety on that beach, we had to explore, and that meant climbing up and over the mountain. That's how we found you. I know my news is very disappointing to you. Unfortunately, we have nothing to offer you but our good will. At least for now, we consider your island our haven and we hope to make it our home. We'll work hard to help you and your community. We'll try hard to be worthy neighbors for your Fellowship."

Chapter 10
Isaiah

Friends or Foes

As usual, Jethro was the one to begin the post-mortem, which was inevitable after the shock we had all received that morning. Only one subject was on our minds: how to approach future relations with our new unexpected neighbors. Jethro was concerned it might lead to an unpleasant breach between various members of their own Fellowship. He worried about his brother's negative attitude toward the newcomers, and he knew Horace had his own legion of followers.

"Here are the facts: They do not have a ship, they did not come here to rescue us, and this is highly disappointing. I am as upset as anyone. When they arrived, I thought it would only be a matter of a few weeks before we would start packing up our whole community to begin our long-awaited move to a future home. Now I realize I was guilty of building castles in the sky. Thinking back, it's clear they never said a single word about a ship or about rescuing us. We just believed what we wanted to believe. Isaiah, you've had more contact with them than any of the rest of us. What do you think?"

"I actually like everyone I've met, but I must say, they had many opportunities to correct our impression they came to our island on a ship. They never said a word about their actual situation until this morning's meeting! Cleary, they made a decision to keep that from us. I can't figure out why. And, if they kept it from us when they first came, knowing we thought they came on a ship, why did they change their minds and tell us their whole story this morning. It puzzles me. They seem like quite decent people, and obviously very courageous. But can we trust them? The old man, John, appears to care for his people and wants what is best for them, and his son Carl, who delivered the bad news this morning is a pleasant guy. He laid it out for us this morning. They're not nasty people, none of them. If we believe everything Carl said, a natural disaster did them in and forced them to leave their home. They all feel they're lucky to be alive. There is no doubt in my mind he believed everything he said."

Horace could not wait to get his two cents in. "Thanks, Isaiah. I knew I could count on you to think they are all wonderful people. I don't agree. I don't know what their game is, but it seems pretty clear to me it is not an honest one. Their story is too preposterous. We have to believe in an island swallowed by the sea, in a bridge that appears and disappears, and that somehow they built rafts out of logs which carried all fifty of them a huge number of miles on a rough sea in a wild storm to land here, on our sanctuary island. Preposterous!"

Horace continued his characteristic rant. "I'm not sure what, if any part of their tale is true, but even if they are telling the truth, the presence of an extra fifty or so people on this island presents us with some very serious problems. Will we have enough food for everyone? Where will they live? What will they do to earn their keep? That's just scratching the surface. And I'm sure they have things stored where they landed on the other side of the mountain. I have no idea what's there. And it might be perfectly innocent, but then again, it might not be. I say we've got to do everything possible to get them off this island rather than continuing to treat them as honored guests."

Jethro interrupted. His upset with his brother was written on his face as soon as Horace started to speak. "Horace, have you forgotten who we are!? Are you suggesting we throw them off the island and back into the sea, men, women and children without a chance in the world of surviving? All on the basis of your vague suspicion that they have some sort of evil intention toward us? You have to admit they have not done one thing that indicates any evil intention toward us or this island. Is that how you think we Believers should behave toward strangers? Is that how you and I were brought up to think and act by our parents?"

"I didn't say that. As usual, you're twisting what I said. I think we should talk to the old man and his son and explain to them how tight things are here. Everything here must look great to them. They've got to understand how careful we have to be with our food supply. They don't know how close our whole community came to starving to death on a couple of occasions during two of the last three winters. Things are good for us now, but you know it is not always this good and that is precisely why we want to move to a more secure and civilized world. If we explain it to them like that and they are the kind of people you and Isaiah seem to think they are, they'll understand and be willing to move on as soon as they can."

"So you see, I'm not such a tough guy. I'm not really suggesting we throw them in the ocean, but they did say they have a couple of rafts back where they landed. After they have had a few days to recover and get organized, we can give them some of the remaining planks we have stacked in our storage shed and help them build a couple of additional rafts. We can suggest they pick a calm day and sail to another island or figure out how to sail back to the mainland. If they are as resourceful as Carl indicated they are, they will accept the challenge. After all, when they leave here they won't be any worse off than when they arrived. My point is we can't just absorb all of them. We do well to take care of all of our own people. We don't need theirs too."

Chapter 11
John

A Plan for the Future

I could imagine the conferences taking place among the Believers. We were also in the midst of an earnest conversation following the big meeting. Gunnar and Mal had come to our tent to join Carl, Zoey, Rachel and me. Naturally, we were discussing the impact Carl's disclosure might have had on their hosts. We also needed to establish a strategy for the immediate future. "I watched their faces when you were telling them our story of how we happened to wind up on their island. Jethro looked positively stricken as he absorbed what I was saying. Isaiah, who I really like and who seems to be the number two man around here, also looked surprised, but he didn't take it as hard as Jethro. The one I'm worried about is Jethro's brother. His face looked like a storm had just broken, and I felt as though his eyes were shooting darts at all of us as you finished speaking. I don't know how important his opinion is, but he is Jethro's brother and certainly his opinion matters. When you finished speaking, just about everybody in that building started talking at the same time and it was beginning to sound like bedlam. The prevailing mood was definitely dark. Things quieted down only after Jethro pounded his gavel over and over again and finally was able to adjourn the meeting. They went their way and we went ours. That was not such a good ending. I don't know what it's all going to mean, but we all knew they would be upset, and obviously they are."

Zoey spoke up next. "Carl, only did what he had to do." She turned to her brother. "I'm sure none of us blame you, Carl. We couldn't let them go on believing we were going to be their saviors. They'll adjust to the reality, they'll have to. We're here, and they have to figure out how they want to treat us." Zoey stopped and there was a momentary silence as they all seemed to be waiting for some pronouncement or policy statement from me. My only thought was that we must clear the air and reestablish friendly dialogue right away.

"Carl, I want you to find Jethro and Isaiah as soon as possible. Since you are the one who dashed their hopes and expectations, you should be the one to assure them they have nothing to fear from us. It is important for you to emphasize that we understand this is their island and we consider ourselves their guests. Assure them we will do everything possible to lessen the burden our presence puts upon them; that we will willingly work under their guidance and, that all the time we are here we will exert our best efforts toward escape from this island, not just for our people, but for them as well. After you talk with them, you should have a meeting with Horace and try to create a friendly relationship with him. Make sure he understands we have only good will toward him and everybody in their Fellowship. Try to slip in the word Fellowship whenever you can. It will help convey the message that we heard and appreciated everything we learned about their Fellowship as well as their situation on this island. Try to create a relationship with him personally, the kind of relationship that says to him that the two of you can work together to make things better for everyone. It is so important for us to diffuse any possible enmity as early as possible." I then asked for suggestions from Gunnar and Mal Abrams.

Mal responded, "I guess you are right that we need to be as conciliatory as possible. After all, we are outnumbered about two hundred to fifty. If it ever comes to the kind of conflict where numbers matter we're up the creek. But John, I must say the idea of Carl getting chummy with that brute Horace doesn't appeal to me at all. No matter how friendly Carl can get, I wouldn't trust Horace for a minute. Remember how he practically snarled at us when he brought us to the tent area, and he kept using the word temporary about the tents? What I heard him say was the tents won't be here very long and neither will you. It seemed pretty clear to me he wants to get rid of us as soon as possible."

Gunnar decided it was his turn. He ignored Mal's concerns and turned to me. "I agree with everything you said, but I think Carl has got to do more than just reassure them we mean them no harm. He's got to go with some positives; something more than simply accepting and making the best of the status quo. "Carl, I think you can talk to them about us having skilled manpower. You know we do. We can build our own houses. Tell them we will come up with ways to communicate with the outside world. I don't know how yet, but we'll figure it out. Ask if they have any old instruments stored away, any old motors, any kind of sound systems they rescued from the ship when it went down, any kind of projection equipment or computers. Explain to them how things worked at Serenity Cove, how through the years we kept reaching new people who came to live with us, though nobody could really explain how we contacted them. Let them know we had something magical happening, and that maybe it can happen here. All they know about us is how we had to escape from the island. They have no idea how positive and magical it was all of those years. We have to let them know we're something special, not just some unfortunates who were unlucky enough to land on their island."

Gunnar's positive attitude sparked everyone's imagination. Our little gathering went from a somber assessment of our predicament, to building a plan for the future. When he finished speaking it was as though he had given us a shot of energy. I looked around and everyone seemed to be standing up straighter and there were smiles on their faces replacing what had been worried frowns. I think we are more ready now to look confidently to the future.

Chapter 12
Carl

Let the Chips Fall

I was well satisfied after my talk with Jethro and Isaiah. I was confident that I had accomplished my diplomatic mission well; that they now understood we meant them no harm, that we were prepared to work with them, and that we felt strongly our relationship must be amicable. I was considerably less confident I had achieved any kind of understanding with Horace. Before we even met, Horace insisted he must have a friend with him for the meeting. I wasn't against that, but I wondered why he was so adamant about it.

I met Horace and his friend James down by the port, and was relieved the meeting started graciously. Horace seemed somewhat apologetic about his requirement that he have an ally with him at our meeting. He explained his friend James was there to accurately report our conversation to the elders of their fellowship. "Sometimes I get accused by certain people of saying things I didn't say and meaning things I didn't mean. If there is any disagreement about anything they always paint me as being the belligerent one. I trust James to be a reliable reporter. He has excellent hearing and an incredible memory."

"Thanks Horace. I do understand. I too am aware of the need to satisfy my elders, particularly my own father who suggested I meet with you one on one. We knew you would be upset when I told you the actual circumstances which brought us here, and that we did not come by ship. I appreciate it was upsetting to you, to Jethro and to your entire Fellowship, who were looking to us as rescuers, to suddenly find yourselves responsible for a bunch of strangers. We knew you'd be upset when you learned that we don't have a ship, or any way of communicating with the outside world. We understand your apprehension and will do everything possible to work with you for the common good."

"Carl. I appreciate what you just said, but perhaps it is in my nature to worry about what you haven't said. You held back on important matters before, and we wonder what you may be holding back still. We worry about what you may have hidden on the other side of the mountain. I worry that you may have armaments there. I worry that you arrived here as though by magic. I worry that you may have a strategy for taking over this island. I worry there may be more of you on the other side of the mountain or perhaps on a ship waiting off shore for you to report about us before they join you in an attack. So, you see, I have my worries. Admittedly, none of these are serious concerns, but I do have to think and plan as though they are possibilities until I am positive your intentions."

"Your presence does create a one very real concern. We will have serious difficulty feeding all of our people, and your people, too, once the summer growing season is over. Only time will tell how things will work out between us if there is a serious food shortage."

"Yes, you judged right I was upset after that meeting and I'm still upset. I am upset that my brother foolishly believes everything will come out right in the end. He sees only good. He is a dreamer and I want to protect him and the rest of our lofty idealists. This island may not seem like much, and it's true we would like to leave and find a more civilized world out there; we also can't lose everything that is precious to us. Our people have been talking about escaping from this island since long before I was born, but this is our home. It's all we have, and I mean to protect it. So, take it from me, Mister, if your people came here with the idea of taking over this island it's not going to work. If I ever see you or any of your people posing any kind of threat, I will be there to see you don't get far. That's all I've got to say. And I'm saying it just to clear the air so there won't be any misunderstanding between the two of us. I don't want to hear later that I was antagonistic to you. I'm being very courteous. I'm just telling you the way I see things. James here is my witness that I didn't say or do anything threatening. I've talked enough for now. As head of maintenance, it will be my job to improve your living conditions. While I'm in the process I'm sure we will have many opportunities for the two of us to exchange views again.

"Horace, you've told me what's on your mind. Thank you for being frank. Now I want to tell you what's on my mind. I get it that you are the man who makes things happen around here, and I look forward to working with you. For us to work effectively together there's lots I'll need to know. For instance,

I want to know more about that ship your ancestors were on, the ship that went down so many years ago. How far off shore was it? What did they manage to salvage from the ship and what might still be hidden away on it, things we might still be able to resurrect and use to benefit all of us. Can you to show me every bit of machinery, engines and communication equipment you have stowed away here? And, my friend, since you obviously still doubt what we have told you about our arrival on this island, I invite and challenge you to climb around to the other side of the mountain. I'll ask two of our good climbers to accompany you as guides for you and as many people as you would like to have accompany you. That way, maybe some of your questions will be answered. You'll be able to see everything we left on that small beach. You'll see our smashed rafts, our extra clothes abandoned on the beach, the pieces of sails my sister Zoey was trying to sew together to make a tent to shelter us before we realized there was a way around the mountain and we wouldn't have to stay on that beach. I want you to see it for yourself, and I hope that will satisfy any question you may have about how we wound up here and that we have neither hidden weapons nor secret plans."

He took me up on my offer. He sent word to our tent that night after our cook-out dinner, that he was ready to tackle the mountain. I called my two stalwarts, Joe and Sandy who had gotten me around that mountain on our exploratory climb. Both were eager to be the expedition leaders for Horace and his small entourage.

They started out early the next morning, after gathering provisions for the climb. Dad, Zoey, and I walked with them to the start of the path and waved them on their way. It wasn't clear how long it would take for them to climb up and around the mountain, examine the beach to Horace's satisfaction, and make it back to the starting point.

Jethro had appointed a small group to wait through the day and night for their return. Among those were two of the Believers' medical people, an old man they called Doc and a young woman named Missy, who was introduced to us as a nurse. Dad, Zoey and I walked back to our tent for the night.

At first light the next morning, Zoey and I returned to the base of the mountain. I was anxious to see Horace and the team of climbers return happy and unbruised, hopefully satisfied by their challenging two-day exploration. It was mid-morning when we spotted the six of them coming around the bend, high above us on the side of the mountain. I could see Sandy leading the line and assumed it was Joe bringing up the rear. It was easy to spot Horace. Though he was smaller than either Sandy or Joe, he was much taller than his compatriots. Two of them seemed to be limping, but apparently none were seriously hurt. We started waving to them, but they were not looking our way, more concerned with stepping safely since the part of the ledge they were on was still very narrow. Eventually, someone spotted us and they all waved happily back. At least it appeared they were all waving happily. As they got closer to the bottom and we could see each person clearly, it became obvious that in contrast to his fellow travelers,

Horace's face was shrouded by a dark scowl. Sandy was the first to touch flat ground.

"Welcome back! How was the climb this time?"

She surprised me by rushing over to me, giving me a big hug, and whispering in my ear. "He's really pretty awful. It would have been a fun climb without him."

She didn't have to tell me who she meant. She quickly pulled away from me, and helped the first of Horace's group down the last couple of steps from the ledge to the ground.

"Welcome back, everyone. How did you find things on the beach?" I addressed my welcome to all six of them. By now they were all on the ground. The Believers were being tended to by their medical team, Doc and Missy. It seemed they all had sore feet and sore hands. The two who had been limping had cuts on their feet which needed to be wrapped. Joe answered me in quite a loud voice. His intention seemed to be not to just answer my question, but to make an official statement he wanted all of the Believers to hear.

"It was pretty much the way we left it. I was embarrassed we left the beach in such a mess. There was one positive change, which might be significant. The water level was much lower, and there was a lot more beach! The climb went fine. We did have to help a few of our friends over the boulders, but we expected that and they were good sports about it. We used the rope and did some pushing from the rear with them just the way we did for you, and the way we helped all of the older folks on the same route." I laughed, remembering my own discomfort. "Thanks Joe, a good report. You can tell me more later. Now I'm going to go over and see what they thought of your adventure."

James became spokesman for his group. "That was quite a climb! I don't know how you did it with all your people. And you carried so much with you over those huge boulders and along the ledge. I don't know how you did it. Sandy and Joe felt the need to apologize to us that the beach was left a mess. Then they started to clean up. I think they were planning on bringing more back here with them until they realized how much help the four of us needed just getting to the beach; and we would most definitely need just as much assistance on the return trip. They made a neat pile of clothes and things under the tent you all put together there." James' report certainly sounded positive and admiring.

Horace spoke up next. "Well, it looked pretty much the way you said it would look. It was a perfect picture of a beach after a shipwreck. You did a good job there. I do thank you for sending along those two kids. They were both very helpful, particularly Joe. The girl Sandy was a little snippy at times, but I guess she was okay." Then he switched topics. "I'm disappointed Jethro isn't here. He should have come back with you people to meet us. That's the least he could have done! After all, I am his brother. I suppose he thought he did right by us just sending along the medical team, such as they are. Luckily, we didn't have any serious wounds for them to tend to. I think I'm done answering questions for now. We're all pretty hungry and tired, and we still have to walk back to town."

Chapter 13
Jethro

Integration!

"Yes Jethro. It looked like they showed us everything there was to see. That's the way it looked, but we only had a few hours and I got the feeling they were keeping us as far as they could from the area where they had stacked the intact rafts. From the contours I saw of the cliff at that point, it looked like there might be caves behind those rafts. I want to get back there without any of those people escorting and showing us what we should see and keeping us from what they want hidden. I bet they have stacks of weapons in those caves. I don't trust them for a minute. That Carl always sounds so reasonable. I'm convinced he's just a good actor. Every time the man tells me something, I get the whiff of dishonesty oozing from his pores. I tell you, I know I'm right, and I can smell it. If I go back there the way I suggested I'll find the evidence to prove it to you. What do you say to that? I'll take one strong guy with me to help with the climbing and I'll crack open all of their lies and show them up for what they really are."

Isaiah and I sat dumfounded listening to Horace's tirade. "Horace, you've been reading too many of those old books. You're starting to resemble one particularly disagreeable character. Do you remember the captain in the book "Caine Mutiny?" I think his name was Captain Queeg. You sound paranoid, just like him. Remember in the book, he dreamed up a conspiracy about some missing blueberries? Stop and think what you just said. I can assure you, Carl and his father and their whole clan did not come here to steal our blueberries, or anything else. What do we have that they would want to steal? There is nothing here to steal!"

"You're right. They didn't come to steal blueberries. They came here to steal the whole island from us. There's something valuable on this island, something they knew about when they set sail with this as their destination. That's why they're here."

"Horace, listen to me. These are good people. They are not here to steal our island. They are just the victims of some very bad luck. It's our job to help them. The Bible tells us we must help those in need, and these people are in very great need. They've lost their homes, and arrived here with nothing but the clothes on their backs, and the will to live. They need our help. Just forget about going back there to find evidence. I believe the evidence of my eyes and ears, and I am convinced that these people are exactly who they say they are. Now, either you're going to agree to work with them and help them, or I'll have to put someone else in charge of maintenance and another person in charge of community relations. You've been my reliable right-hand man for years, but that can't continue if you keep dreaming up these crazy theories."

"You think I'm talking crazy do you? Ask James. He was with me. You think they sent those two kids along to help us.

Yes, they helped, but they also sent them along as watchdogs to make sure we didn't stumble onto things they want to keep hidden. And that girl, Sandra, I swear she was trying to seduce me. She kept brushing up against me, trying to drive me crazy. I think she was trying to distract me so I wouldn't be interested in looking around. I resisted and it wasn't easy, but the fact is she did distract me. If I wasn't on God's mission to uncover the truth I might have fallen. James will tell you they were keeping things from us! He probably saw her making advances too. Even if he didn't see that you can believe me, it happened. James will back me up. Your friend John Johnson is a schemer and his son Carl is not to be trusted. James will tell you. Just check with him. I know he'll tell you the truth just like I've been trying to tell you for the last half hour. "I need to go home and get some sleep. You just talk to James and you'll learn I've told you the absolute gospel truth."

"Horace, go to bed. Sleep is the best idea for you right now. You're over-tired. While you're napping, I'll have a chat with James and the three of us can talk again later, after you've had a few hours to relax. So, sleep well, Brother. I'll see you in a few hours."

James was surprised and not at all happy being summoned by Jethro. His normal mode was to remain quietly in the background, helping where possible, rarely taking the initiative in creating a project or even in leading a conversation. When Jethro questioned him about their expedition around the mountain, he did not hesitate to give straightforward answers.

"No, Jethro. I didn't get the feeling that anything was being hidden from us; in fact, it all seemed very much in the open. It was clear they left that beach in a hurry, and didn't have time or the ability to carry all of their things. As for the rafts, there were three of them, pretty much smashed up, broken beyond repair, and two that looked like they could sail again except that their paddles had apparently floated away and their sails were torn."

James looked genuinely puzzled by the questions about Sandy. "No, I didn't see Sandy rubbing against Horace. In fact, Horace called her over several times to help him get over obstacles. You know Horace doesn't make friends so easily. He is suspicious of everyone, but he seemed to really like her and wanted to keep her nearby, ready to help at his beck and call. Both of those kids, Sandy and Joe seemed like super athletes and very agreeable kids, as helpful as could be. I talked to Joe for quite a while, and he glowingly described the island they had to leave. He said they all loved it there and were devastated when they had to leave because the tides were about to drown them."

"I also asked him about John, their leader. He said John had been in charge all of his life, and nobody ever had a bad word to say about him. Then we got on the subject of the rising water and how they wound up here on our island. He said 'John saved our lives, saved all of us, insisting we should build those rafts and not depend on our cars getting over the bridge. None of the other resort leaders agreed with him. I think everyone else from Getaway Island died. We watched from a distance as the ocean washed up and over their cars. All of them must have died. It was terrible! We're the only ones left and we have John to thank for the fact we're here.' He didn't sound like they had any plan at all about this island. They couldn't even navigate the storm. He was just thankful they had survived."

"Thank you, James. I know you and Horace are good friends and this was difficult for you. When he asks us about this conversation, which I'm sure he will do, we will not discuss what you told Isaiah and me. What you did tell us is a bit worrisome. He's my brother and I love him. I would appreciate it if you would keep an eye on him for me. I'm concerned that he's just not acting himself lately. I want to make sure he doesn't get into any unnecessary conflict with our new friends."

Chapter 14
Carl

Time to Build

I had a pleasant surprise the following afternoon when Horace and James came to the Johnson Family tent and offered to lead any who were interested in a visit to the storehouse where materials were located, the materials we would need to build housing for ourselves. Dad and I were interested to see what they had, and Dad had me run to the Svenson and Pollard tents. I came back with both Gunnars, Senior and Junior, and with Harry. Off we went with a surprisingly subdued Horace and James.

As he led the way, James adopted the dual role of enthusiastic tour director and authoritative island historian. Horace, usually so talkative, came along with very little to say. It was an unusual role reversal. While we were walking, I could not spend too much attention to wondering about their relationship, I was only focused on what we would see and discover.

"We're almost there. The warehouse is on the edge of the forest close to the port. I'm told, the men who built it were a few of our original shipwrecked Believer brethren. Of course, it is hard to know exact history since everything we know has been filtered down to us through three generations. Some stories must have changed with time, but I do believe it is likely those original men constructed this building."

"Here's the story as I know it. Horace, please correct me if I make a mistake." Given the opportunity, Horace couldn't remain silent another minute.

"You already did make a mistake, the serious mistake of questioning our history. All of the people before us were God fearing men, and they were scrupulous with the truth. I'd better tell our history to make sure they hear it straight."

James seemed to clench his lips together and force himself not to respond. Horace continued, "The official story is that the hold of the ship that went down was filled with building materials for the houses they planned to build when they got to Greenland. Our Fellowship researchers had assured the leaders at the time that Greenland was quite an empty land. As Jethro explained yesterday, the ship never made it to Greenland. When the storm hit and the ship went down, it was apparently fairly close to the Southern coast of this island, where it eventually settled not far below the surface. After they realized that almost everyone had survived the shipwreck, next came the realization that they were apt to be marooned here for some time. The better swimmers actually dove underwater, and were able to explore inside the ship while it was all still together in one piece. They were able to rescue some important materials from the ship's storeroom. The most significant materials were those they needed to build housing. They stacked most of the stored lumber and gathered up all the hand tools, lots of nails and bolts, and they started to build. We still have the saws, the planes and chisels as well as the hammers and nails, but of course, most of the original lumber supply was used up. I'm told the construction was a long difficult process since so few of the men were handy with tools. And, of course, none of the women were allowed to help.   First they built housing. Then they went to work building the piers we use to this day as our fishing platform. After they completed the housing and the piers, they got to the storeroom. The ship must have gone down in the Spring and all of this construction was completed in the few short summer months."

"By the time they got to the storeroom, construction materials were running out, consequently, it's not as large or complete as it should be. Since the building itself couldn't be very large, it limited how much more material they would be able to salvage from the shipwreck and store for future use."

When we arrived at the storeroom, Horace led us in with apologies. We soon saw why. It was immediately obvious the remaining lumber supply would not build very many houses. We only needed five more large houses for our five families or perhaps ten smaller ones if we could build a house for each generation. It was at this point that Harry Pollard couldn't resist telling Horace and James about the properties of the incomparable White Bark Spruce trees, and that we had observed a few of those same trees scattered through their forest.

"Of course, it may not work the same way on this island, but on Getaway Island when we cut one of those White Bark trees down another started growing in its place almost immediately. So, we never ran out of wood. When we learned the sea was going to inundate us, we ran out of time, not wood. The bark of those same remarkable trees can be planed down into sheets of very strong, very thin material. That's what we used for sails. Those are pretty versatile trees, they're a valuable asset. After we finish here we should see if there is one of those trees close by. If so, we can show you both what we can do with them. The only tools we'll need are a medium rip-saw, a sharp knife, and a plane."

Horace looked skeptical at first and then increasingly interested by Harry's enthusiastic description. A few minutes, later the seven of us had gathered up the required tools and were headed into the forest. It turned out we found a White Bark Spruce less than twenty-five yards from the storehouse.

Gunnar Sr. spoke up. "Hand me the saw first. I want to show you how you must cut these trees so that we do not injure any of the wood." He got down on his hands and knees. About six inches above the ground, he started a diagonal line across the bark down to ground level on the opposite site. "Now stand back." We all moved back and he started to cut along the line he had drawn. He cut half way and the tree fell neatly, leaving a clean diagonal stump. Now just watch." As we all stood and watched, we could see new sprouts coming out of the tree stump. Within a half-hour a new tree was growing. Horace and James were astounded. The rest of us had observed this phenomenon many times in the weeks before we fled, but it was a fascinating sight. It never got old no matter how many times it was observed.

Then it was Harry's turn to take over the demonstration. He took the sharp knife to the fallen tree, and started to lift the bark off, as though he was peeling a piece of fruit. He went around the tree, around and around until he had a sheet about six feet long. Then he cut across it. "Now, if I take this sheet into your warehouse and plane it down, I can get three thin sheets from a single piece of bark. It also takes ink without tearing or blotting, I can print on it! I'll show you how whenever you like. I'm sorry Zoey isn't here now. She's my best printer. She could probably explain the process better than I have."

Horace's mouth was hanging open. He was clearly impressed. "I have to get Jethro and show this to him. James, would you find Jethro and get him to come here. Just tell him it's something terrific for him to see. He's been doing a lot of worrying lately. This will be a great surprise for him. Don't tell him anything. Save the actual surprise until he gets here and sees for himself. He's got to see this. This is simply remarkable. Now I understand how you could make rafts and sails that allowed you to travel so far loaded with people as you most certainly were. How did you ever discover how to do so much with these trees?"

James came back a few minutes later not only with Jethro, but also with Isaiah, his wife Leah, their two children and James' own wife Sonia. There were soon exclamations of surprise and excitement from the assembled group. Only Jethro stood looking without saying anything, he was imagining all of the possibilities. There was a lot of chatter and cross conversations going back and forth. Together we were now quite a large group. When Jethro did speak he addressed himself directly to Dad, who he viewed as his opposite number among the newcomers. There was a notable lull in all of the side conversations as everyone was interested in Jethro's reaction.

"John, that tree that your boys just cut down, how long before it can be made into usable planks for construction?" John deferred to Gunnar.

"I could have five ten-inch-thick boards for you by this time tomorrow, that is if there is a good saw in that shop of yours. The wood takes almost no time to cure once it's cut. But the best part is the new tree growing from this very stump will already be about eight to ten feet by tomorrow and will be full grown by the next day. So, in terms of construction, lumber will certainly not be a limiting factor. The real issues will be the right saws and skilled carpenters to do the work. My son and I can work together and we had been training Jack Abrams before we had to leave the island, but we could use more good carpenters if you have any."

Horace spoke up. "That's my department. I certainly know how to use a saw! And I've been using little Jimmy as my helper on home repairs. He's been learning all the skills we need to keep our cabins from falling apart. They were built a long time ago, and they're just wood, not magical wood like these incredible trees. We have to do a lot of repairing."

John asked Jethro if they had ever thought about making

rafts to get away from shore to see if they could locate exactly where the ship went down. "When you told us about the original shipwreck and the survivors diving down and rescuing equipment, it made me wonder if you have thought about doing anything like that lately? It's a fact that things sitting on the bottom of the sea do shift from their original locations. You could send two or more rafts in slightly different directions each day until the remains of the ship are located. Then some of your best swimmers could go down and explore."

"That is an intriguing thought. There has always been a rumor, and it probably is just a rumor, that there was something of great value in that ship that has never been brought ashore. I actually remember asking my grandfather about it, and he gave me a very vague answer, as though he was even embarrassed to discuss the subject. He said the ship had probably shifted and was no longer located where someone could swim down and retrieve anything from it. I was intrigued by his answer, and I asked him again a few months later. He got angry with me and said I should never talk about such foolishness ever again. I never did bring it up again. I had forgotten all about those conversations until now. I wonder if there is anything of value sitting there at the bottom of the sea."

"It would be interesting to take a look. After we build a few cabins for our people, maybe we should start building rafts and do some exploring. I appreciate the fact that the addition of our people is creating a potential food shortage. We want to help, and I think if we go exploring we might come up with something which will ease the food shortage. I feel guilty enough imposing on you as we are. And maybe we can even locate the remains of your ship, and get down to it and explore. All of our young people are enthusiastic swimmers, and they'd love the challenge and the sheer adventure of it. I bet some of your teenagers would also enjoy doing it."

"Well, they might, but I would be surprised if many of our Believers are strong swimmers. The ocean has always been viewed as both mysterious and dangerous. This sentiment dates back to the fact that our presence here on this island is due to a shipwreck. Most parents I know have actually discouraged their children from going into the ocean except in very shallow water close to the beach to cool off on the very hottest days of summer.

Isaiah, who had been very quiet since observing the demonstrations of the White Bark Spruce trees, spoke up for the first time. "Jethro, you might be surprised at how many of our people really do go in the water and swim. You're rarely down by the port so you haven't seen them. I don't want to shock you, but I have occasionally seen your son Elijah swimming in the deep water, swimming laps between the two piers. I think John is right. Some of our people would look forward to helping locate that ship as an adventure. My children are too young, but I bet they would leap at the chance if I said they could."

Chapter 15
Carl

The Discovery

"I'm sure it was the most exciting day on the Believer's Island since the day we arrived. They were all out there. They stood on the shoreline, the entire community, clapping, cheering, singing; flags fluttered in the breeze, bands played, families picnicked on the beach, all as though at a joyous festival. Many were there expecting to witness an instant miracle. In fact, what was about to happen was the first attempt at a search for the remains of the ship, which they hoped would be found resting under the water not far from where they stood cheering. It was the start of a quest that was bound to be lengthy and might not prove fruitful. The actual players were young. Zoey's and Hank's son, Mark, Jack and Sandy Abrams, Richie and Joe Westfall, Horace's son, Henry, and James' daughter, Olivia were the divers, the seven of them ready to launch their two newly crafted rafts. They knew it was serious business, but to them it also sounded like a great adventure. Their parents, better informed than most, stood on shore with all of the others, hoping for some proof positive of the location of the legendary sunken ship.

The rafts had been designed by Gunnar for their specific purpose. He had built oarlocks to hold the paddles in place so there was no possibility of losing them if the rafts were ever swamped or while their occupants were searching under water. Each raft was designed with two distinct sections, a passenger section and another larger reinforced area to carry the treasures they hoped to bring back with them from the ship. On shore, the scene resembled a giant treasure hunt, a game for big kids, seeking a buried pirate's treasure. Nobody knew where it was hidden, and nobody had any idea whether there could be anything left after so many years under water which might still qualify as treasure.

A great cheer went up from the crowd as the two rafts pushed off from shore, headed into the ocean in slightly different directions. Sandy was designated captain of one raft and Joe the other. Both teams paddled a fair distance away from shore, perhaps seventy-five yards out, before there was any indication from either of them that could be discerned from shore. At that point both rafts paused, and simultaneously one member of each crew stood and dove off the side of the raft. The crowd held its collective breath waiting for them to re-emerge. When a minute or so each of them broke the surface, there was an expectant hush on the beach, followed by a disappointed murmur. Both divers signaled that they had found nothing. The rafts now moved to new positions, each about fifty yards from where their first dives took place. A second member of each raft team now stood and went over the side. They came up empty-handed as well. The procedure was repeated several times to the obvious disappointment of the beach crowd, a large number of whom appeared to lose interest and started to slip away back toward their cabins. But the parents of those involved, and many others as well, stood rooted to their shore-line positions watching every move.

It was late afternoon when Joe came to the surface, climbed up on his raft and clapped his hands overhead. He had discovered something. The crew of his raft started lowering a Gerry-rigged anchor. It was an enormous clumsy looking rock encased in a hemp canopy attached to a long rope. Sandy's raft was paddling furiously their way. When her raft reached his, they lashed them together. We all observed them conferring on their newly combined rafts, which now resembled a decent size platform.

Sandy and Joe dove off the platform together. They went down, came up a minute later. They sat for a while catching their breath and then went down again. When they emerged for the third time, Sandy came up waving a piece of a tattered flag. Joe came up with what looked like a piece of railing. They were excited and so were their team members, who started happily hugging one another and jumping up and down until they suddenly realized they risked tipping the rafts. That brought them quickly back to reality. They tied a floating marker to the rope that was attached to their improvised anchor. The two rafts separated, and both crews started paddling back to shore.

The seven exhausted but happy young divers were immediately surrounded by parents, grandparents, brothers and sisters and leaders of the Believers. We all wanted a first report on their quest for the ship which until that moment was thought to be a myth to the current generation of Believers. Our Serenity Cove group, Dad, Gunnar, Harry, Zoey and the other refugees were thrilled knowing they had found the ship. We were now convinced the wrecked ship was accessible enough to explore. We now felt justified in having expended the time we had spent organizing the venture and the enormous effort we all had exerted finding and cutting down the widely scattered White Bark Spruce trees. It had taken both time and effort sawing and finishing the logs into boards and finally into salvage rafts. In addition to the construction, it had been essential to create and train the diving teams, all in a few short weeks. Dad and the other leaders were convinced that there was more to be found in the body of that ancient ship than the original Believer group had brought to the surface all of those years ago.

Jethro called a "round table meeting" to discuss the subject that was on everyone's minds and lips. The meeting was to take place in the Meeting Hall. Jethro designated himself, Isaiah, Horace, James and Doc as the Believers' representatives and suggested to Dad that he appoint four others as "Serenity Cove" representatives.

Dad designated me as leader of the Serenity delegation instead of himself. He did this understanding that he risked insulting Jethro and others by designating me since I represented a younger generation. In fact, Dad felt I was more capable than he might be at this point in our respective lives. He didn't want to over-represent our family by including himself in the group. The others he chose were Gunnar, Harry, Mal and Sam Westfall.

The big hall, which I had last seen filled with people, now seemed vast and empty. The ten members of the newly formed round table were seated in a semi-circle in the middle of the room. Facing them, seated in a row were the seven young heroes of the day. Jethro banged an actual gavel on the small desk which stood in front of him.

"We are here to congratulate our brave explorers, who risked their lives today to attempt to answer the question that has plagued our Believer Fellowship since their early days on this island. Has that ship whose journey ended in disaster remained where it went down? Will we be able to find it again should we ever want to do so? And, perhaps most crucial of all, are there still objects on that ship which can be salvaged and restored in condition to benefit our community? The first two questions have been answered with a resounding affirmative due to the courage and skill of our young diving crew." He turned to them smiling and clapping. The others took up the applause. He continued, "Now we would all like to hear first-hand a report from the two of you who actually made the dives that brought you in contact with our goal."

When the applause died down and Jethro regained his seat, Sandy and Joe stood. Sandy spoke first. "It was an honor to be chosen and so much fun to go out on those rafts. The last time we were on rafts we weren't sure we would survive. We thought we were going to die. This time as we climbed on our minds were occupied by hopes for success and without any fear. Carl had worked out a chart for both of our rafts, indicating the direction and distance we should move the rafts each time we needed to search a new location. He also trained all seven of us on breath holding. We trained together in the port area, going under water and staying under as long as possible. Carl had us do this over and over until we could all stay under at least two minutes. Today, when my raft got to the third location we still didn't see anything, but when I saw Joe's signal I knew a diver on his raft had spotted something! Joe and his team held their position, waiting for us to reach his raft. When we did, he and I conferred and decided we should be the ones to go down as far as possible. When we dove we both saw the ship far below. There was no question, it was the perfect picture, there was the ship sitting right side up on the bottom. We pushed ourselves down as far as we dared to see if we could grab something to bring back to show. The center mast was the highest point on the ship. I tried to take the flag from the top of the mast, and it tore in half in my hand. I came up with the small piece which you all saw. That's all I can tell you."

"It was like Sandy said. Visibility was good. The ship was clear and was well below us. We only got down as far as the very top of the mast. I grabbed what I could. I think the rail I brought back was part of a ring high on the mast that was like a safety hatch for the sailor whose job it was to sit high on the mast to spot obstacles. I think that lookout post is called a crow's nest. As I said, most of the boat was still below us. I thought I could swim down to the deck, but was afraid I might run out of breath before getting back to the surface. So, I broke off that piece of railing to have something to show. It may take more breath training before we can get down to the actual deck and spend any amount of time there. I hope I'm one of the people who gets to go back to explore further. It was the most exciting thing I have done in my whole life."

The next few days I was down at the port every afternoon, working with the dive teams. Sandy's team, which only had three divers (herself, Richie Westfall, and Zoey's son Mark) had a new addition, Jethro's son Elijah. I was somewhat surprised when Elijah appeared for a tryout, and, before letting him join the class, I asked Jethro if it would be permissible to use Elijah if he proved capable. Jethro had sounded so negative about swimming, and clearly was unaware that his own son had become an advanced swimmer without his knowledge. Whatever went on in the privacy of their home, it soon became clear that Elijah was not only an experienced swimmer, he was also a better dive candidate than any of the original group, except possibly Sandy and Joe. In their workouts, I didn't actually have them attempting deep dives. Instead, I concentrated on having them swim laps under water to improve their ability to expend effort while holding their breath. They practiced for about an hour a day; each day the entire group got better and better on underwater breath holding.

After they had been working at it for a few days Dad came down to watch me in action as a coach. He was also happy to see his grandson Mark, the youngest in the group at age sixteen, working hard as one of the dive team. Every so often Zoey would drop by, staying out of sight as much as possible to watch Mark work out without him seeing her. I think she was also surprised and pleased to see me in my new role as swim team coach.

While all of this activity went on at the waterfront there was constructive action on land as well. The goal was to build five new cabins, each large enough to house multiple generations of the Serenity Cove families, and to complete them before the winter weather set in. Late fall and winter would make outdoor construction progressively more difficult the colder it became. It was agreed that the Serenity Cove people would be the only ones working on the cabin project. Dad told me Horace was 'displeased' that he was not put in charge of the construction. He felt that as the resident maintenance director, he was being passed over. Apparently, he had burst into Jethro's house, and demanded a change in policy. He was not happy to find Dad there. Jethro assured him he was indeed crucial as head of maintenance.

"You already have plenty on your plate with fifty or so aging cabins to take care of. You'll have plenty to do this winter without getting involved in construction for our new residents." Horace seethed when he heard Jethro's designation of the 'newcomers' as new residents. This was rubbing salt in his wounds. He still thought of them as intruders.

Dad tried to further soothe Horace's ruffled feathers. "Our people are presenting enough problems for all of you folks just by being here, and the least we can do is construct our own housing with as little additional work from you Believers as possible. You have been incredibly generous to us and we appreciate it, but it's time we start to take care of ourselves, at least as much as possible. Fortunately, Gunnar and his son have lots of experience with this type of construction."

In fact, Gunnar and Gunnar Junior had already created the design for a new model multi-generation cabin, fashioned with a goal of privacy for each of the married couples, a common dining room and a large play area for the young children. It was a great design, but a little more complex than the simple cabins they had lived in at Serenity Cove, and definitely more complex than the Believers' current cabins. Actual construction work would start as soon as they had the materials they would need.

Harry called his team together. He said he had a proposal for a project that could be of great importance. His team was a small one. His son Alan was his right- hand man, and Zoey enlisted her husband Hank as part of this new team. So, there would be four of them working together.

"We are all aware that Carl has been working with the divers to improve their ability to stay under water when they go back out to try to search the ship. I applaud Carl for his efforts, but realistically, how long can they be expected to hold their breath, maybe two or three minutes, and that will hardly be time enough for any real undersea exploration. I propose to create and fashion a workable version of a deep-sea diving helmet." He paused, waiting to hear all of their reasons as to why it could not be done. He knew it was easier to come up with the reasons it would not work than to figure out how to make it happen. He had thought it through, and was convinced it was possible. He waited, but there was no response. They sat in silence, not quite believing what they heard.

Zoey was convinced as soon as she heard it that the idea was nonsense, and she was saddened to think her boss and co-worker of so many years, was growing senile. She was trying to think of how to reply negatively without upsetting him too much. Just as she was about to respond, he continued.

"Here's my idea. I know it will not be like a real diving helmet, usable multiple times, but each helmet can be used one time to extend the breathing time to five or possibly eight or ten minutes for a single dive. We can ask Gunnar and his team to make a frame that will fit over the diver's head and tightly around the neck. We will use the thin but very strong bark from our favorite tree, bend it to create a large bubble to fit the shape of the frame. I'm sure you know how flexible that bark can be. Ah, but you are thinking what is the missing ingredient? How will they be able to see through the bark? And, even if they can see through the bark, how will that expand their breathing? I have the answer to both of those. Working with care, we can scape a portion of that bark, thinner than we have ever scraped it before, thin enough to see through. That portion would be in front of the diver's face. It will not give perfect clarity, but will allow the diver to see. When it gets that thin the bark is also going to be very fragile, but the ability of the diver to see is vital. The helmets must be handled with care. That clear shield should last for at least ten minutes in the water before it becomes cloudy and loses its clarity."

"Now, you will ask yourself how this will enable the divers to breath. The answer is here in the forest. You know there are no actual topographical maps available, or at least we have never been shown one. I've been wandering through the forest doing my own mapping and looking for our missing ingredient. We all know there is a source of good fresh water here on the island somewhere. We've been drinking it since we got here. Of course, I could have just asked Isaiah where the source is located, and he would tell me, but I wanted to do a little exploring on my own. If I failed to find the source I could always go back to Isaiah and ask. I did go looking on my own, and I found it. I knew there had to be a well or a pond somewhere. I found the pond, a clear pond at the foot of the mountain, well North of where we came down on that mountain path. The pond is bordered on one side by the sheer cliff, but on the other side there is a sort of marshy area. On the edge of that marsh, I found just what I hoped to find, tall reeds! I cut a few of them just to see if they are hollow, and they are. We can cut a big bunch of the reeds, sew or somehow glue them together, end to end. Then we need to drill a narrow hole in the front of the shield of each helmet, insert the reeds and, voilà! we have our breathing tubes. I know when we put it all together the whole affair will be very flimsy, but if everyone who handles them is very careful, these tubes should allow each diver more time than a diver with no assist at all." He paused again waiting for a reaction. "Now, what do you think?"

Zoey smiled to herself. Well, I guess he hasn't lost it completely. I doubt if it will actually work, but I do agree it is worth a try. We'll see how far we get before we run into a snag that stops the whole project dead. She kept silent, waiting to hear from the others. Harry's son Alan started clapping, and they all joined in. "Dad, that's great! What a great idea. I bet it'll work. When can we start?"

Hank congratulated Harry on his creative thinking and said he would be willing to work on it, and hoped that it would turn out the way Harry imagined. Zoey smiled again. Her husband didn't disappoint her. He was always conservative in reaction to new thoughts and new ideas; but he was always open as well, ready to see if the new idea was workable. She knew this would be a fantastic experiment and nobody, including any of us, could possibly tell whether it would work or not. But it was Harry's idea and when we get it all together we'll test it out. Even Harry agreed it is a long shot. I listened to their reaction and certainly felt it was worth a try. If it does work, it will certainly enable my divers to explore longer and better.

Six weeks passed since the first dramatic diving session, and once again we stood on the shoreline, the entire community, clapping, cheering, singing; flags fluttering in the breeze, bands playing, families picnicking on the beach, all as though at a joyous festival. This time, many of us on the beach were better informed. A very few expected to witness a miracle, but most of us were waiting and hoping, not knowing what to expect. Everyone knew the two diving teams had been practicing their diving and breath-holding skills day after day. This time, we could all see preparation had been very different. The rafts were populated not only by the divers but also by a carpenter. This time, the each raft had been reenforced to hold equipment and had a stack of clumsy looking diving helmets sitting on the deck. Each raft had one additional passenger as well. Horace was on Joe's raft and Gunnar Jr. was on Sandy's. They were there to supervise and assist with any equipment or material the divers might be able to salvage. Joe's team was made up of with James' daughter Olivia, Jack Abrams and Horace's son Henry. Sandy's team had a new recruit, Jethro's son Elijah, along with Mark Blake and Richie Westfall.

I was on the pier. I gave the signal and the divers paddled their rafts out toward the marker they had left marking the ship's location. Once again, they tied the two rafts together, and two divers from each raft struggled to get into their new diving helmets.

Sandy and Elijah secured the helmets over their heads, checked to make sure that the breathing lines streaming behind them weren't tangled, jumped in, and swam toward what they hoped was the bow of the ship. Their goal was to find and get into the command bridge to see if there was any kind of equipment that could be salvaged. They were happy to see the water was relatively still and clear that morning. Sandy pointed the way and Elijah followed close behind.

Later, Sandy gave her account of what she saw. She made

her way unerringly to the remains of the bridge. It was defined enough for them both to be sure that they were in the right place. They swam through the wooden doorway, jostling it as they went through. The attached door separated from its hinges, collapsed and seemed to disintegrate as it fell to the deck. As they entered the bridge, they could see the captain's wheel still intact, but at an odd angle, as though it had detached and was hanging by a thread. They were just turning toward the back of the command cabin when Elijah tapped Sandy and made a chocking signal. His breathing line had become blocked. He floated out of the cabin, and started swimming up toward the surface. Sandy followed, but before she left the command bridge she had the impression of some kind of instrument mounted or possibly hanging from the rear wall of the cabin. She was halfway to the surface when she realized her helmet was filling rapidly with water, that her breathing tube had detached. She had a moment of panic, and then her breath-holding training kicked in, and she was able to hold her breath while completing the swim to the surface. Both Sandy and Elijah emerged and floated toward their raft. The other divers pulled them onto the raft, removed their helmets, and helped them collapse down onto the deck, where they lay panting.

While Sandy and Elijah had been swimming toward the bridge, the other two divers, Joe and Jack dove down toward the stern. They were hoping to find an open hatch that would take them further down into the hold of the ship where all of the materials and equipment had been stored in preparation for the passage to Greenland. Joe was the titular leader, but it was clear to both of them from their numerous practice sessions that Jack, like his sister, was a very strong swimmer, stronger than Joe. Jack led the way in their descent. First they passed the area which must have been passenger cabins. A moment later they were on the main cargo deck. It was empty. Jack spotted an opening, and they both swam down the open hatch into the darkness and gloom of the hold. They looked, but couldn't see anything. It seemed to be a vast empty space, with no obvious structures or stored materials. They swam around side by side hoping to locate something, anything. After a few minutes searching they both knew their breathing tubes were providing only a slight bit of air, while at the same time they were expending precious energy. They knew the tubes were closing and they would have to hold their breath as they made it back through the hatch and up to the surface. When they did reach the surface both of them were as exhausted as Sandy and Elijah had been. They needed help from their crew in getting helmets off and assisting them to flop down on deck until they too could return to normal breathing.

Once they caught their breath, it was time for a conference right there on their combined rafts. The four divers compared notes, while Gunnar Jr., Horace, and the carpenters listened in. Collectively, they decided the same four divers would go back down when they felt ready, and that all four would head toward the bridge together to see if Sandy's fleeting impression of some instrument might prove to be real. and, If so, it might take all of them to dislodge it and bring it up to the surface.

As they sat conferring, suddenly the calm sea beneath them became agitated and very bumpy. It was a moment of panic for them and for us on the beach. They grabbed onto each other and stretched across both rafts to hold them together. A wave suddenly lifted them, and just as suddenly let them down into a hollow. They breathed a collective sigh of relief as they watched an enormous whale breach and swim peacefully away as the seas around their rafts became calm again.

Stacey asked, "Do you think we should go down again or wait until we're sure that whale won't be coming back this way?"

Elijah responded. "I remember the story of Jonah. I say we wait at least five minutes, and if the whale doesn't come back, we dive again. We may be close to saving something really valuable. Who knows how long that thing you saw will stay where you think you saw it. We may have dislodged it some just by going in there. Let's go get it!" It was decided. The four divers each selected a new helmet, checked the breathing lines and were ready to dive again.

Sandy led the way with her twin brother, Jack, right behind her. It was agreed they would enter the cabin through its doorway, while Elijah and Joe would come through what had been the window. Their main concern in entering the small bridge was to keep the multiple breathing lines from getting tangled. Elijah had a surprise for them. He pulled a strong flashlight from his pocket and shined it toward what was obviously some sort of instrument on the wall. Although it wasn't very large, all four of them crowded together in tight quarters trying to get their fingers around the edges. It was actually easier than they thought. As soon as their fingers dug behind it, the wood that held it in place fell apart, disintegrating into tiny particles, and floated away. Elijah and Joe had the rather slimy apparatus in their hands, and started swimming out the front window. The four divers all headed toward the surface. They all experienced the same collapse of their breathing tubes at just about the same time, but were able to continue swimming upward, holding their breath while their slimy prize was brought to the surface. Hands reached out from the raft to pull the instrument onto Sandy's raft. A few minutes later they were all on the raft and their breathing was returning to normal. The unidentified treasure was slick, encased in green algae with bits of the plywood protruding irregularly. There was no question in any of their minds they had brought up some important instrument or it would not have been secured on the captain's bridge.

They signaled their success to us on the beach. They all stood up on signal, Gunnar Jr., Horace and the eight divers, hands high in the air, they clapped and then pumped one another's hands in exaggerated congratulatory handshakes to give a clear message to those on shore that an important discovery had been made. The sound of cheers reached them from the beach, confirming for each that they had just completed a heroic adventure.

Before they started to paddle back to the pier, Sandy and Jack turned to Elijah, and Sandy asked, "Where did you get that flashlight?"

Elijah looked puzzled, and then he realized what she was asking about. "Oh, you mean the magic candle? My father said he found two of them years ago in one of the corners of a store room in the meeting house. Nobody knows where they came from or what makes them light up, but they are very useful."

Sandy knew about flashlights. Her dad had one he had taken from his car. His didn't light up anymore because the batteries were dead. She couldn't understand how the batteries in Elijah's flashlight could be alive for so long. She asked to examine it. She tried to unscrew the bottom and the top, but quickly discovered it was all one piece and heavier than she imagined it would be. "No matter how it works, it sure is useful. If we go back out again make sure you bring it with you."

I was so excited they had found something, I could hardly wait to see what it was. Once they were actually back on shore, and we could all see the prize they brought with them a more serious and troubling question remained. What is this thing and will it be of any actual value?

Chapter 16
Interested Observer

Still Searching

Gunnar looked down at the curious object laying on his work bench. He was not alone. He would have preferred to work alone, with just Junior helping him. Still, he understood the enormous interest in this strange object that had been salvaged. Junior stood by ready to assist. Of course, Carl was there, intending to both observe and to report back to his father. Three of the divers also asked if they could watch what they thought of as the unveiling of their treasure. Jack and Sandy Abrams were looking on curiously, as was Elijah, who was probably there both because he was one of those who rescued it from the depths, and also as a representative of his father. The instrument now sat on the work bench. Beside it was a rectangular white metal tray. In the tray there were several cutting tools, an oddly shaped pair of pliers, and a few things that looked like ladles. Next to the tray were two bowls. On the floor just below the bench were two buckets.

"Junior, you do the honors. Start by cutting away the outer layer of seaweed."

As Junior started peeling away the greenish seaweed, a gaseous stink seemed to permeate the area where they all stood. The outer layer of gloppy stuff was shoveled off the bench into one of the buckets below. They could almost see through the messy stuff that now surrounded the object. It was hard to make out details, but as they cut off the outer layers, the shape of a box became clear.

"Very careful now. What you have to do is peel the next layer off rather than trying to cut it off." All eyes were on Junior and the oddly shaped pliers he was using to peel down to the core. A corner emerged. They could see a black top. The front had a murky glass covering, something that looked like it could be a sort of chart. As Junior continued peeling layers of vegetation away from the box, Jack and Sandy worked next to him, cutting off the cleared material, and shoveling it down into the buckets on the floor. The peeling and cutting continued until it was clear they were looking at a black box. The top, bottom and both sides of the box appeared to be sheet metal. The face of the box was a glass screen. Poking through the metal box below the screen, there were four knobs.

Gunnar turned to his helpers, "It's clear we are looking at some sort of a radio here. Judging from where you guys found it, this may have been the ship's radio. Chances are good all of the works inside are corroded and useless, but we have to wipe every part of this very carefully to determine if we can do anything with it."

"Carl, why don't you let your dad know what we have here. You too Elijah. I'm sure your father will be very interested. Jack and Sandy, thanks for your help. I think it will be best if Junior and I continue working on this alone. We have to be very careful and it could take a long time. We'll let you all know just as soon as we can tell what we actually have here." Carl was slightly affronted by the dismissal, but decided not to say anything. The other three grumbled audibly as they left the shop area.

Gunner and Junior continued work. They had a bowl filled with a liquid that smelled like alcohol and were dipping the corners of washcloths in and then wiping the box, and particularly the glass face, as clean as possible. The wiping was slowly giving up more information as they worked. They discovered that the entire back wall of the box was removable. It was held in place by four tiny screws. The screws were entirely rusted, and as soon as they touched them with screw drivers they broke. Gunnar then easily removed the back of the radio. The two of them sat looking at a profusion of tubes and wires, all of which had been soaking in sea water for the past fifty-plus years and could not possibly be of any future use. On the very bottom of the radio they found a metal plate with the manufacturer's identification, which would contain the company name, model number and perhaps other information as well. Gunnar wasn't sure it would be particularly useful information, but he wanted to know everything he could about their treasure. He and Junior continued rubbing to clear the plate, until finally letters and numbers started becoming legible. The largest lettering was the name "Hallicrafter Radio Company". Below that they were able to make out "model S-38-B."

"Junior, I remember the name Hallicrafter! They used to

make short wave radios and ham radios. They were a very important company during the war, and for a while after. I wonder if they are still in business. Wouldn't it be nice if we could just pick up a telephone to call them, give them the model number on this box and tell them all of the parts we need to replace."

"Dad, while you're dreaming, why not just dream this was a ship to shore radio, that it still worked and that we could use it to call for help." They continued cleaning, shifting their attention to the glass screen that formed most of the front. Letters started emerging. They could make out the letters WEEI... WBZ.... WHDH.... WNAC... WMEX. After looking at them for a while those letters started to ring a bell for Gunnar. He explained to Junior these were the names of radio broadcasting stations back in the old days. "When you were a little boy, before we ever lived at Serenity Cove, we used to have a radio that looked a little like this one. It sat on the kitchen table and we would all sit near it and listen to the news and music and sometimes even stories on our radio. When we moved into Serenity Cove we eventually forgot all about listening to the radio. There was always so much to do. Nevertheless, I sure wish this one could work now."

"I don't see how hearing the news from America can possibly help us or the Believers ever get off this island. Even if we can get it going and can hear the news from the rest of the world, nobody out there will know we are here waiting to be discovered and rescued."

"Junior, my hope is that this is a two-way radio and that we can somehow make the thing work again. I don't know how yet, but I'm going to try!"

"Dad, one thing that's been on my mind since everybody has been talking so much about trying to get off this island and go home... have you thought where we and the others Serenity Cove people should go? Will we all go back to the towns you all came from before you found Serenity Cove? It's been so long since any of you were there, would it still really be home for you? For the people my age those places you came from don't mean anything. America, Boston, Baltimore, Philadelphia, United States, are just words, and for our children those words mean even less."

"I'm sorry they mean so little to you, but I understand what you are saying. You must know from what we have told you that none of our families intended to leave our homes in America. America was and is our country. Every one of our families was just going on a vacation. It was a combination of luck and magic that had us wind up at Serenity Cove. The places where we lived in America were pretty pleasant places, and, yes, it would feel to us like we were going home, no matter how many decades have passed since we were last there."

"It is possible that we may never contact anyone using this radio, but even so, some day, a ship is bound to stumble on us here on this island. We can't be that far off the coast of Maine. This island must be shown as uninhabited on nautical charts. They don't know anybody lives here, but some day they are bound to come exploring these 'empty' coastal islands and find us. If and when a ship does come, it will almost certainly be from the United States. If they have room for us on their ship, my hope is that they would take us back to America. After all, that's where we all came from. Of course, for the foreseeable future, it seems highly unlikely that there will be any rescue. For our own sanity right now, we should plan as though we will be here on this island for an indeterminate time?"

"What we really should be concentrating on is not how to get off the island, but how to make things better right here. We need to concentrate on how to solve the food problem, and how to integrate our two very different communities. Working on this radio is an intriguing challenge for me and I have my hopes. Realistically though, it's unlikely to get us anywhere. We are destined to be disappointed if we count on being rescued anytime soon. This island may not be paradise, but it seems like a sufficient place for us to live."

While Gunnar and Junior continued cleaning and speculating about the radio they had in front of them, Carl, along with Stacey and Jack, made their way back to their Serenity tent. Carl immediately reported to his parents, Zoey, and his brother-in-law Hank, on the identification of the mysterious box as an old-time radio. Gunnar and Junior had been working on it when he left, so he had no idea whether it could ever be made operational. John was surprised that Gunnar had already been able to identify the nature of the box, but nonetheless wanted to switch the conversation to what was on his mind.

"No matter what kind of radio that turns out to be, we shouldn't lose sight of two other important avenues we should look into. The first is to search the hold of that ship again. I know the original report on the exploration of the hold revealed nothing, but there were only two people looking and they did not have a flashlight with them. Until Elijah brought a flashlight on his last dive, I don't think any of us knew that there are flashlights on this island. I suggest we send another exploratory group down into that hold with as many flashlights as possible to see if there was anything we missed. That means our divers should have more practice sessions to prepare to go down into the ship again.

"The other thing we really have to do is conduct a thorough search of the storage area in the Meeting House. When Horace showed us around, I saw lots of boxes piled in a dark room, presumably all things salvaged by the original team of Believers right after they arrived on this island. When they were originally recovered, they were soaking wet, but were not then corroded or worthless. In all the years since, they may have deteriorated into total junk. Hopefully, some may still be in usable condition, and perhaps we can figure out how to make use of them."

As Carl reported Gunnar's limited findings to his family, Elijah had hurried to report his observations to Jethro. When he opened the door he was surprised to find a house full of people. His parents were hosting Isaiah and Leah and children as well as Horace and Esther. They all listened attentively as Elijah made his report. He knew they were anxious to hear if anything worthwhile had been discovered. After he said everything he could think of, they all sat quietly, perhaps waiting for more. Was his report disappointing to them? He hoped not. He thought it was pretty important that they at least knew the nature of the box he and Joe had so carefully carried to the surface from the submerged ship.

"Thank you, son. I'm glad you were there to see and hear what they have determined is a radio."

Then Horace also gave thanks in his fashion. "Yes, thank you Elijah. I'm glad you were there. But it doesn't sound like those two really accomplished much. Did you get any sense that Gunnar and his son were holding back information? Do you think he asked you all to leave when he did because he didn't want to share what they might learn, that he and Junior wanted to keep certain information to themselves?"

Before Elijah could respond, Isaiah broke in angrily. "That's not fair Horace. Do you expect Elijah to always be suspicious like you? He's only eighteen years old. Why is it that you are always looking for bad motives? From what Elijah has said, it sounds like those two were working as efficiently as possible and maybe thought they could work faster if they didn't have a whole group standing looking over their shoulders. I've seen you working at that bench occasionally and you are always quick to shoo everyone out so you can work undisturbed. That's what their dismissal sounded like to me."

"I just don't trust them. I've said it before and I'll say it again. I don't know what they are up to. I don't have any idea what their plans might be, but I'm pretty sure they don't take into account what is best for us."

Jethro decided the contentious interchange should come to an end. "I do want to remind you, Horace, Elijah was not the only one asked to leave. So were Carl and the Abrams twins, not just Elijah. Let's end the conversation about motives and think about what has been learned. I personally think it sounds like they have unfortunately run into a dead end. A radio that was under water for years, that was, as far as we know, only a receiver not any kind of two-way radio, is unlikely to be of any use in getting us off this island. The question is whether there is anything else we can do now that the ship has apparently given up the last of its secrets."

Elijah jumped in. "I'd be willing to go explore the hold again with either one of the Abrams twins. They're both great swimmers, much stronger than me. We may have missed something in that hold because we could not stay down long enough to get close to all four corners. I'd like to go back down again, with a flashlight, and get a little closer to the two corners we only saw from a distance. There might be something else of value down there."

Later that day, John paid an official visit to Jethro. "Well, Jethro, we have progress of sorts, but you know as well as I do that that radio will not get us in contact with the outside world unless it can be fixed. It doesn't change the situation much unless there are other parts floating around in the ship, or possibly in your storeroom, which can somehow be adapted to work with it so it can do more than just receive broadcasts. Gunnar is asking for permission, to search your storage area with Horace or whoever he chooses to see if there is anything there which can be used. What do you think?"

"Done! I'm sure you know Horace is protective of his territory, but I will propose it to him as a dual exploration. He can hardly say no."

"That's great. I'm going to propose something else too, this with a good deal more reluctance because of the danger involved." Jethro interrupted.

"I know what you're about to propose. My son has made the same proposal, that we conduct one more diving expedition to attempt a further inspection of the hold. I've always wondered what else might be down there since my grandfather seemed so reluctant to even discuss it with me. I told Elijah I would propose another diving expedition to you. "

So, the two leaders having agreed, another dive was in the works. Things looked very different this time. Gone were the crowds standing on the shore. Nobody was there clapping, cheering, singing or waving flags. There were no families picnicking on the beach and there were no bands playing. Another attempt was about to be made to find anything left of value still hiding in some dark corner of the sunken ship. There may not have been large crowds this time, but the parents of the divers stood nervously on shore with a good number of people from both groups who realized there was still the potential for a major find.

Stacey and Jack were there, along with Elijah and Joe. They were standing by their rafts, ready to take off on another diving quest. This time all four were planning to simultaneously enter and explore the hold. They had carefully mapped out areas they wanted to search, very aware that they must keep their breathing lines from tangling as they all planned to enter and leave through the same narrow open hatch on the main deck.

Carl gave the signal and both rafts took off in the direction of their anchor marker. When both reached their spot they again fastened their two rafts together and prepared for the dive. Elijah and Joe jumped off first. A minute later, Stacey and Jack plunged down and out of sight. Very carefully, they all made it to the deck and then down through the open hatch. Each team had a flashlight this time, and each team was assigned two corners of the huge hold to explore. Elijah and Joe had the longer swim to get toward the front of the hold, the area which had not been reached on the previous dive. Stacey and Jack took the rear corners. They did first one corner and then the next, already feeling their breathing lines starting to close. They shined their flash all around and saw nothing but walls.

Elijah and Joe spotted an unusual shaped box in a corner. As they swam toward it the oddly shaped box became identifiable as an old-fashioned steamer trunk. It took a huge effort by both of them to lift the trunk out of the muck which had accumulated around it. Once they got it off the floor they were able to carry it surprisingly easily back to the floor just below the hatch they had dropped through two minutes earlier. By the time they got to the opening, they both sensed their air lines were closing so they worked as quickly as possible. It took a much greater effort pushing and pulling to get the trunk up and through the hatch onto the deck. They left it there. They had no choice. They were both running out of air. They swam up toward the surface.

On the raft, Gunnar and Junior pulled Stacey and Jack up onto their raft. Horace and James did the same for Elijah and Joe. They all flopped on the deck, breathless. A few minutes later they were able to start breathing normally and they related the fact there was a trunk sitting on the deck down there they would have to go down and retrieve. Elijah said they had no idea what was in the trunk, but it was pretty heavy as they brought it up from the hold onto the deck of the ship. He did think that two of them should be able to get it to the surface...since they wouldn't have to expend time and air searching around before they got to it. They could go straight down and bring it up.

One hour later, the divers and all of the observers were back on the beach, all crowding around the sealed trunk. They could hardly wait to see what was in it. Horace and Gunnar both had pry bars, and, with a great effort, the top finally released its hold on the main body of the trunk. They stood and stared speechless when they saw what they had uncovered. The trunk was filled with items of incredible wealth.

It was a dazzling display. On the top tray there were sterling silver bowls and vases, and table flatware which appeared to be solid gold, twenty-four karat gold forks, spoons and knives. After all of the initial oos and aahs, these were carefully replaced in the tray, and it was removed and laid out on the sand. The next layer down was filled with solid gold platters and plates. They were lifted out in stacks and carefully laid on the beach. Below them there was another divider. They removed the divider and found smaller lined compartments overflowing with diamond necklaces, dazzling jeweled brooches, pearl earrings, diamond, emerald and ruby rings and, at the very bottom, stacks of strangely imprinted gold coins. It was incredible to think all of this wealth could have been carefully accumulated and then packed by members of the Believer Fellowship who had left New Hampshire on their journey to Greenland so many years before. This must indeed represent all of the hoarded finery and wealth of generations of Believers from long ago.

For the longest time, nobody said a word, they were dumbfounded. Elijah was the first to speak. "Dad, we're rich! This is a fortune! I never knew Believers could be or ever were ever rich."

John and Gunnar, Carl and Zoey stood shaking their heads in wonder. Jethro, Isaiah and Horace were even more astonished. In all of the tales told to them by their Elders, nobody had ever mentioned a trunk full of actual treasure. There were no tales of fabulous wealth, no stories about members who were rich as Croesus, never a word about a fortune possessed by the Fellowship. This was a shock in every way. From the time they were young children they had been brought up to believe that superior knowledge and good deeds were the only real wealth. There had never been a word about the kind of wealth they saw lying at their feet and all about them on the beach.

Jethro had a very private thought he chose not to share, but couldn't quite get out of his mind. He thought this was what his grandfather didn't want to discuss with him so many years before. But why? Why was it such a secret? I never knew why he got so angry with me.

Finally, John broke the spell of silence. "I know you Believers are just as surprised as we are to see the contents of this trunk. I just want you to know that we from Serenity Cove will never make any kind of claim on this spectacular treasure that was just uncovered. We know those items all belong to the Believers Fellowship. When we are all rescued and free to leave the island, I personally pledge that no members of Serenity Cove will ever lay claim to any part of that fortune. We wish you well, now and always, and hope that all of your members here will someday be able to enjoy the fruits of what has just been rescued from the deep."

"Thank you, John. I appreciate that even though the thought had not occurred to me that you would do or think otherwise. Elijah, this find does not mean we are rich. It just means we have found riches from the past, riches that we may never have the opportunity to enjoy. You and the other divers have done wonderful, courageous work diving down into that ship and rescuing that trunk. Everyone on the island appreciates your courage as well as the courage and hard work put in by so many others, particularly so many of our new friends who have been working so hard on our behalf as well as their own. John, Carl, Gunnar, please accept my wholehearted thanks."

They very carefully repacked the trunk and closed the lid. Four men, under Horace's supervision, carried the trunk to the Meeting House. Horace decided the best and safest place to secure the trunk was right in the middle of the floor so that any time anyone came or went into the Meeting House, they would pass it. And all eyes would be on it at all times. "This", he said, "is the most secure place of all. Nobody will dare touch it."

That day and the next the incredible treasure trunk was the main topic of conversation everywhere on the island. It was so hard to process that their Believers ancestors had such wealth, and even harder to believe they somehow missed salvaging that trunk with all of the other items they did rescue from the ship. This immediately became the favorite subject in every quarter, but it was soon joined as a topic by something less exciting and more important to everyone. This was the report Gunnar and Junior made, first to their Serenity Cove people and immediately after to Jethro, Isaiah, Horace and all of the Senior members of the Believers. Gunnar was very careful to use the same words when speaking to the each of the groups.

"There is no question this radio was used on the ship as a substitute for a real ship-to- shore radio. It is called a ham radio because hams are what they once called amateur broadcasters who communicated back and forth on such radios all over the world. Ham radios were very popular but did not have the reliability of dedicated ship-to-shore radios. What we have here is a ham radio built by the Hallicrafter radio company, model number S-38-B. Unfortunately, the interior was sitting in a salt water bath for so many years that it's hard tell if there is any way to make it work. Junior and I have removed the back, carefully removed all of the tubes from their sockets and untangled several feet of wire. That leaves us with many unanswered questions. First is whether the tubes are damaged, even though they look fine superficially. Next question is whether the years of being underwater has created gaps within the wires that are not visible. Then the biggest question of all is whether we can find or improvise something that will serve as a microphone so that we can speak to the world as well as hear from it. It is my hope, Horace, that with your help, we can search through the contents of the many boxes still piled in the back of the Meeting House. You say the original Believers tried to rescue everything of value and store it, but left no inventory of what was in all of those boxes. Perhaps we will be lucky and find just what we need to make our radio a viable way to connect with the outside world."

John and his family and all of the other Serenity Cove people were excited and hopeful when they heard Gunnar's report. John responded for the group.

"Great job, Gunnar. You too, Junior. Congratulations on doing what you have done. How long do you think it will take to dry out all of those wires and tubes to see if they can still be made to work?"

"Hard to tell, but they are laying out on benches next to our tent, baking in the sun right now. We'll keep checking on them, and at some point we'll have to make an educated guess as to whether they are ready to test or not. There is one more problem, a rather large one, as far as I know there is no electricity on this island. Without that, there is no way to even test what we have. I wish we had that generator we left back in the main cabin in Serenity Cove."

With Gunnar's last statement, John's hopes disappeared. He knew all about the importance of the generator. For all of the years he was in charge, he had kept their old generator going with their limited oil supply to power the computer. That was how they communicated with people who later joined them and became members at Serenity Cove. He had forgotten about the absence of electricity, the absence of a generator, the absence of a computer. How stupid of me, he thought. I can't believe I forgot the most important item of all. My mind is not working the way it should.

"Gunnar, is there really any hope at all of using that radio?"

"Probably not, no hope at all unless we can find a generator and a source for oil. I consider both of those highly unlikely, but I don't want to give up yet. Who knows what's buried in those boxes they have stacked in the back of the Meeting House. Our divers struck gold, literally. Maybe we'll get lucky and strike gold, too."

Chapter 17
Zoey

High Hopes

We were fortunate to have reached this incredibly promising moment. Many of us were gathered around the work bench, the largest assembly on the island since that first time when everyone had gathered on the beach to watch the divers. Gunnar was director of this project, and the focal point. Sitting on the bench, carefully cradling the radio in both of his big hands, he was ready to turn the switch to "On." Junior sat next to his father, carefully holding the end of the wire to the stub of a power cord he had discovered in the lower corner of the radio box. Harry's son Alan held the shaft of an outboard motor in a vertical position to keep it off the ground. I had been given the dubious honor of pulling the cord to start the motor. Elijah was standing by as back-up to me, and Jack Abrams was his back-up. Jethro stood just behind Gunnar with a very small microphone in his hand, connected to the radio by a thin copper wire. He was ready with the important speech he had memorized. He had been accorded the honor of being the first islander to speak to the outside world. It was his job to call for help. Isaiah stood next to Jethro ready to take over in the unlikely event that Jethro might suddenly lose his voice. Yes, we were very fortunate to arrive at that moment, but it didn't just happen. Many of us worked for days to reach this critical moment.

The first unexpected break was the result of Horace's remarkable memory for something he recalled seeing when he was a child playing in the forest with his friends. "I don't really think it will be of any use to you, but I thought I should mention it. I had forgotten all about it, but I'm pretty sure it should still be there. After all, there is nobody around here who could or would have used it."

"Lead on, Horace! We can't afford to ignore anything that might offer the possibility of a power source." I was the only woman on this outing with Horace. Carl and some of the others leaders didn't think it would be worth their time.

"We're pretty close now. This is the only part of the whole forest that has undergrowth and weeds. I have no idea who would have dragged it to such an inaccessible part of the forest. I only saw it that one time when I was a kid. I'm pretty sure it had a kind of motor on the back. It's a vague memory, but that part is pretty clear in my mind. I'm sure it was a motor. It can't be far now. The bushes are getting thicker and thicker. I remember the bushes were very thick around it. Careful, there are lots of thorns in these bushes. I guess they wanted to pick a spot nobody would wander into and steal it."

A few minutes later, we came upon it. What I saw was the bottom of a triangular shaped boat; the kind that used to be called a skiff. We didn't have to look too carefully to see a massive irregularly shaped hole torn in the bottom. A healthy crop of bushes flourished in that hole, lapping over so that the entire boat was nearly invisible. I would never have spotted the boat at all if we hadn't been concentrating so hard on finding it. The splintered sides of the boat were very nearly the same color as the weeds around it. There was only one distinctive feature to the boat and it was precisely what we had hoped to see. Sticking out from the bottom of the boat I saw it, a small black propeller attached to a shaft that went to a motor, the kind of outboard motor typical on a small fisherman's boat. Horace's childhood memory was accurate.

" Zoey, Jack, Elijah, let's turn the boat over to see the business end of the motor." Horace's direction made sense, but as we lifted one side of the boat, the motor separated and fell completely away. Fortunately, the motor made a soft landing in a thicket.

"Horace, you got us here. You say you were only here once years ago. Amazing!"

"Well Zoey, it's all in your hands now. Let's clear it out, and get it to Gunnar and his team. I know nothing about motors."

A few minutes later, we were at the workbench. Gunnar was excited when he saw us coming, outboard motor in hand.

"I don't know much about this kind of motor," he said, "but let's hope we can make it work. I do know it won't work unless it still has gas in the tank. With the motor lying on the ground for so many years it will be a miracle if the gas hasn't leaked out or evaporated. So, let's hope for a miracle."

It happened! We got our first miracle! The small fuel tank had not leaked and, remarkably, was nearly filled with gas after sitting in the forest for fifty or more years.

The motor was certainly crucial, but equally important was the need to find or make a microphone. The radio would do us no good unless we could speak through it. Horace again was the key man. Overcoming his reluctance to let outsiders anywhere near the precious boxes that had been sitting ignored in storage for decades, Horace organized a search of the boxes in the Meeting House. The search took the better part of two days and included only a few of us from Serenity Cove. Most of the searchers were the women and children of the Believers. The children were having a great time playing with some of the things they found, particularly in the toy boxes.

Along with a lot of junk, we located a few gadgets and lots of wires and other quasi-promising items. Interestingly, the most useful box of all turned out to be a box of toys. In the box we discovered a child's radio broadcasting kit. It had a small unlikely looking microphone. We were doubtful, but had hopes the tiny microphone could be made to actually work. Again, luck seemed to be on our side. When we brought it to Gunnar, he examined it and said he thought he would be able to use it.

Most important of all was the radio itself. Gunnar and Junior had worked for days drying all of the wires and tubes. They reinserted the tubes into the correct sockets. Then, through trial and error, they figured out which wires went where, and carefully threaded them into place.

At last, we had come to that time, and we were ready. We all knew everything had to work. If any part failed, it would cause everything to fail and we would have to find another way. I know my fingers were crossed.

Gunnar announced the start. "Okay, everyone? Carl, are you ready?

"Yes, ready!"

"On three, Carl, pull that cord as if your life depends on it, and if it doesn't catch, pull until it does. Starting the count....One....Two....Three...Pull!"

He did. He pulled and nothing happened. He pulled again and again. I could see he was getting tired. I was about to offer to take over for him when we all heard a sputter. The motor caught. The motor started and the propeller started whirling about. Gunner turned the switch on the radio to ON! The tubes lit up! It was electric. It worked! Jethro shouted into the microphone.

"SOS. SOS. We are on an island off the coast of Maine near Boothbay Harbor. Our ship went down. 500 People need HELP."

He continued

"To anybody who hears this, we need your help. Stranded on an island ....running out of food!"....... SOS........ We are on an island off the coast of Maine near Boothbay Harbor....Our ship went down..... 500 people need HELP!

Gunnar was the first to see the window of opportunity shut down. He saw the flickering red tubes dimming, and turning black. All of our eyes were trained on the radio. Then we all saw and felt the window closing. Then came the silence, the deafening silence from the ancient motor whose ugly chugging we had cheered moments before. Our hearts sank as our hopes crashed. Was the motor dead? Was the gas tank empty? Would that be our one and only broadcast?

Chapter 18
John

Changes

I must have been particularly tired the day I decided it was time to have The Talk with Rachel.

"Rachel, I've been leading Serenity Cove for a very long time. I'm getting old, and frankly I'm tired. It's hard to believe but we're both seventy-two years old. I'm worn out from worrying about everyone and everything. I'm tired of the crises. I'm tired of the disappointments. If only we were still in Serenity Cove and life was going smoothly, I'd love to keep going. Unfortunately, that's no longer our world. I think it's time for someone else to take the lead. I'm no longer the best possible leader for all of our people. I hate to step back in view of our recent failure, but maybe that failure is another reason to turn things over to a new leader. What do you think, Rachel?"

"John, if you've had enough of the stress I certainly understand if you want to turn it over, but please don't tell me it has anything to do with that failed attempt to radio for help. It would have been a miracle if that crazy patchwork radio Gunnar put together had truly worked. Did you all seriously think it was going to work?

"Yes we did, but I suppose you're right; It was a long shot.

We all had such hopes. I admit that disappointment has something to do with the way I feel now. I think it is time for me to put aside my disappointment, but I think I am clear now, it is time to pick my successor. Who do you think we should pick as my replacement?"

"If you have made up your mind to retire, let the group decide who should be the next leader. If it was up to you, you'd pick Carl or possibly Zoey because you know them best and love them best. Others might resent that. Put it to the group. They may have other ideas."

"You're right. I would pick Carl because he is so smart and he's proven to be such a responsible guy. He's already taken the lead on a lot that has been done recently. Zoey would be a good choice too, if times were normal. She's certainly just as smart as Carl, and she has a very creative mind, but she has enough to do just to take care of her own kids. I don't think she needs that kind of stress at this point in her life, maybe a couple of years from now."

"John, I don't know what you're talking about. Our grandchildren are wonderful; they've behaved as well as anyone could want during this whole ordeal. Zoey can certainly find the time and energy if she decides she wants to take on the leadership role, but the reality is it's not up to the two of us to decide. It should really be a decision by our whole group. I trust our friends to make the right choice. After all, they kept you on as leader all of these years."

Later that day, I called a gathering of the entire Serenity Cove group.

"Friends, I have enjoyed and been honored to be the leader of our people for many years. Some of you are old enough to remember when I was appointed to this position by our beloved Ellen, the founder of our Serenity Cove. I accepted her appointment and you have all seemed happy enough to allow me to lead. I thank you all sincerely for that privilege, but the time has come for a new, younger leader. It is also time for us to adopt a more democratic way of appointing our leader. The floor is open for comments, suggestions and perhaps nominations."

Mal Abrams was on his feet ready to speak just as soon as John stopped. " John, you can't resign, not now, not when we need someone we all believe in and trust to lead and help us through whatever is coming next. You may not have been aware of it at the time John, but I was angry with Ellen when she first turned everything over to you. After all, Jill and I were the longest standing residents, the very first people Ellen had called to the Cove. I let her know what a wrong decision she had made. I thought she should have picked me to lead, but, I must say you have done a first-rate job ever since. We all trust your leadership and want you to continue. This is no time for you to quit."

"Thanks, Mal. I truly appreciate that. Our circumstances have changed, and it is time for a change in leadership. I will not continue as leader. I'm not going to change my mind. Does anyone else have any thoughts about it? Or have a suggestion?"

Sam Westfall stood up. "I nominate Carl. He's been your

backup person during this whole unsettled period, starting just before we had to leave The Cove and Getaway Island." A large number of heads bobbed up and down indicating agreement. Carl stood.

"I am honored, and certainly would like to continue as a backup person for whoever is chosen, but I don't want to be the leader. I've always been more of a doer than a creative thinker. I know two people either of whom would make terrific leaders, Junior Svenson is one, and my sister Zoey is the other. Junior has been working with his dad and mine for years helping to make things happen. As for Zoey, in her own quiet way, she has organized so many projects and done so much for our community. At one time or another she has worked with every one of you and I'm sure you all know what a great person she is to work with."

There was a buzz all around as small clusters of people discussed the choices. It was a bit of a surprise when Mal stood again.

"John I'm sorry that you appear to have made up your mind, but all of the people mentioned would make great leaders. In my opinion Junior, you're a wonderful young man and I'm sure you would make a fine leader, but I think we need a new approach, a two-person leadership team. Carl and Zoey have spent their whole lives learning how to work closely together, and they will make a great leadership team." His statement drew general approval.

I stood up. "Mal, if that was an official nomination, I second it."

"Yes, it is indeed, I nominate Carl and Zoey Johnson as our new leadership team."

Then I asked for further comments and further nominees. Junior stood up to speak and there was a momentary question in my mind if he was upset at being by-passed. He turned to his father, as though they were the only two people in the room.

"Dad, I know you hoped I would be the next leader of Serenity Cove, and maybe one day I would have been. Right now, there is no Serenity Cove. There may never be a Serenity Cove again. We're in a time of transition, a time of hope and a time of uncertainty. The Johnson family have led us and led us very well through the years. This is still their time, and I trust them as I know all of you do. I heartily endorse the dual leadership of Zoey and Carl, and trust the day may be close at hand when they will succeed in leading us home safely." Then he turned to Carl and Zoey, "All our lives you have been like a brother and sister to me. I trust that relationship will continue on until the time comes for us to say Goodbye."

I saw this was becoming an emotional moment for everyone. People quietly sat absorbing and respecting Junior's sentiments. When he was through, there were a few minutes of hugging, kissing, tears, and promises of forever friendship. Zoey moved toward Hank. He met her with a hug and an approving grin. His head was bobbing yes. His lips said "Do it!"

Finally, I was able to call Carl and Zoey the new leaders by acclamation. As simple as that, all of them had accepted the fact of my retirement and that they had new leaders.

Chapter 19
Observer

Discord Among Believers

At the same time an unusually heated conversation was taking place between Jethro and Sarah.

"Jethro, I told you not to get involved in their nonsense. Imagine trying to make contact with America using a child's toy microphone. Can't you see, even now, how implausible the whole thing was? I can't believe those people have you and Elijah and the others following their orders, even Horace, who usually has such good sense! Even he has fallen under their spell. I hope you've all learned your lesson by now and you will be the ones coming up with the ideas and giving the orders. Let them follow you. Remember, we are four hundred Believers and there are fewer than fifty of those Serenade people."

"Sarah, this is not a numbers contest, and they call themselves Serenity not Serenade. They are the Serenity Cove people."

"Well, whatever they call themselves, it's time you call the tune."

"Fine, Sarah. I'll talk to their leader John Johnson, and explain to him that from now on he is to follow my orders. Do you know how foolish that sounds! So far they have done nothing but try to come up with ways to help us and themselves. They haven't been giving us orders. They've been suggesting plans. It's unfortunate the radio didn't work, but there was nothing wrong with trying."

"No, there's nothing wrong with trying, Jethro. I heard exactly what you said in your SOS message. It was a good message as far as it went, but you forgot to say the most important thing. You forgot the reward. You didn't give them any incentive. You forgot all about that fantastic treasure chest we have sitting in the Meeting House. Why, on Earth didn't you mention a reward, a very big reward for the people whose ship could come and get us off this island? You know that treasure won't do any of us any good sitting here. If you offered it as a reward that might have been incentive for someone to want to find our island and rescue us. Not that it matters now. I can't believe you all thought a message on a toy microphone could actually reach somebody who would come to rescue us."

"Perhaps the problem is that you and Isaiah and Horace and some of the others have been content to just sit here forever on this little island. Here, you guys are treated like kings. In the world out there you'll just be ordinary men. Our Fellowship has been stuck here for more than sixty or seventy years and none of you leaders have come up with a single plan to get us out of here and back on route to Greenland, or some other civilized place. Maybe those Serenade people are good for us after all. Maybe they'll get you men to actually start thinking and planning how to get us off this damned island."

"Thank you for your vote of confidence, Sarah. Be sure to tell me when you come up with a really good plan to get us out of here, a plan that has a better chance than the one we just tried."

"You're impossible! You know what I mean. Just take charge the way you're supposed to and let those people know this is our island and they are just guests for as long as we allow them to stay."

"Sarah, we had best stop talking about this now before I get truly upset with you." Jethro walked quickly out of the room, slamming the door behind him and headed toward the Meeting House.

He arrived at the Meeting House, feeling frustrated and angry after the verbal confrontation with his normally acquiescent wife. Horace and Isaiah were arguing just inside the door when Jethro arrived.

"I think we ought to move that treasure chest to a back storage room rather than leaving it sitting right here in the middle of the floor. Horace wants to leave it just where it is. Jethro, what do you think?"

Jethro was not at all in the mood to discuss the best location for the treasure chest, the Meeting House, storage issues, or anything else. He was still seething at Sarah's unfair indictment of his leadership. He snapped back at Isaiah, his lifelong best friend.

"You two decide. I don't really care where the damned thing is stored. There is no good place for it. You can leave it right where it is so people can lust after it every time they enter or leave the Meeting House, or you can hide it away so people will continually speculate where it is and perhaps go looking for it. There is no good solution. I think that chest is cursed and we would have been better off if it never existed. Like everyone else, I was thrilled when Elijah and that other young man pulled it out of the sea. I thought to myself that is like magic. How could such a thing exist in that ship's hold and still be sitting there all these years later? Why didn't they pull it out with all of the other things they managed to bring to shore? And why was my grandfather so angry at me when I asked if there might be anything else down in that ship? Did he know that treasure chest was down there and how it got there? Maybe he wanted it left there because it was tainted; maybe because it was an accursed treasure obtained by our ancestors in some unsavory fashion. I'm sure now it would have been best left to sit forever at the bottom of the ocean."

Horace and Isaiah were both astonished by Jethro's reaction. Isaiah, though taken aback by Jethro's anger, responded quickly. "

Jethro, I have a much more favorable view toward that chest, though I agree it is hard to determine where it should best be stored. When it was opened and we saw what was inside I was sure I knew why all that wealth was bundled together like that. I don't think there is anything at all unsavory about it. Our ancestors were on their way to a foreign land, and had no way of knowing how they would be received. They must have collected all of the wealth of the entire community and placed it in that trunk, ready to use it not only to buy land for the community, but also as a way of gaining acceptance and security. They recognized, as we should also, that our piety and practices are likely to be misunderstood by the outside world. Wherever they anticipated going, and wherever we ultimately wind up when we leave this island, there will always be issues of acceptance and safety. They packed that treasure chest as an insurance policy, and now it is our insurance and should be guarded as such."

"Do you want to know what my Sarah said about it? She said we should have mentioned our treasure in our SOS broadcast as an incentive for potential rescuers to find and rescue us. What do you think of that?"

Isaiah replied at once. "She's right! I didn't think of that, and I'm not sure I would actually mention a treasure like the one in that chest, but offering a reward could be just what is needed to spur people into action. There are dozens of small unchartered islands off the coast of Maine. We can't give details of this island' 'location because we do not know them, but if anyone heard our SOS Calls, the very vagueness of our location may have been discouraging to potential searchers. The promise of a large reward might have overcome that reluctance. We didn't mention a reward, and now with the radio dead, there is no point in discussing it as though the opportunity is likely to recur."

Horace couldn't resist. "Sarah is a little late with her suggestion, Jethro. Why didn't she mention this earlier?"

"I was sure the idea just popped into her head when she said it because she was disappointed and was angry at us, that we hadn't succeeded. She wanted to tell me how she would have found something better to say than what I actually did say. It's too bad we couldn't have had more time on that broadcast before the radio died. There are lots of things we might have added. We knew we could not count on it working for long, and we did the best we could with the time we had. There is no point in indulging in recriminations now, but I do wish Svenson and his boy Junior were able to come up with something better. In terms of the treasure, I guess we really do have to decide where it is best for us to store the trunk for the indefinite future."

As soon as they were sure Jethro was through, Horace and Isaiah both spoke at once. Surprisingly, Isaiah's voice prevailed. "You're right, Jethro. No recriminations, but we do have to plan ahead. I see no point whatsoever in having that treasure chest right out front where it is. I've watched when people come into this room, they can't take their eyes off this chest. It's very tempting. Having all of that wealth sitting right there is like inviting people to just take a peek. And suppose some ship does come along, they are going to send people onto the island to see what's going on. This is obviously the biggest, most important building. They'll want to come in and take a look. There won't be any negotiation and there won't be any incentive. They'll just see that treasure chest sitting there, open it and take what they want."

Horace was not going to give up that easily.

"All right, Isaiah, we will do it your way. We'll put it back in the darkest corner of the back room behind all of the other boxes of junk we have back there. That way it won't tempt anyone except those who have a little larceny in their hearts. The beauty of your idea is, unless we constantly open it to check on the contents, we'll never know if someone has gone back there and stolen a few pieces of jewelry or a few pounds of gold."

"No need to be sarcastic, Horace. You both have good points. I think I agree with Isaiah on this one. I know that every time I have come in here seeing that trunk sitting there it has made me want to open it just to see all of that extraordinary wealth again. It is very tempting. I think it should be moved out of sight, and yes, I do think we will have to check on it periodically."

Jethro felt good about the discussion and about the conclusion he had just reached. It was a welcome distraction for him after that foolish argument he had with Sarah.

Chapter 20
Carl

Where There is Smoke

After a few weeks, the excitement of a possible rescue receded and life went back to normal. The Believers had their lifetime experiences and habits to fall back upon. Each day at sunrise their families gathered for prayer. Breakfast came after prayer and then everyone went back to their normal activities. The farmers farmed, the fishermen fished the wives cooked and cleaned the small family cabins, and the children played with their toys gathered from nature all around them. Then came evening prayers and the family dinner.

For us, boredom became an increasing component of our daily lives. Gunnar and his few carpenters were the lucky ones. They were busy every day, working on new cabins for themselves and the rest of the community. Construction work would continue until all five families were resettled. Already the big Serenity tent was much roomier. The Abrams family, The Westfalls and the Brownstein clan had already moved into their new homes. The Svensons would be moving next, and we would have the whole enormous tent to ourselves.

I made a point of getting together with Zoey a few minutes every day, primarily to discuss the future. We saw collaboration as part of our new responsibility as leaders to keep everyone occupied. Of course, our over-riding concern was trying to come up with a new idea for making contact with the outside world. That goal was constantly frustrating.

One morning Zoey got to our meeting bursting with enthusiasm. She had a brainstorm during the night and could not wait to share her idea with me. "Oh, it's nothing spectacular, Carl, but I think it is worth doing."

"Okay, you have my attention."

"Since we tried to reach the world with the radio SOS, and the radio died so quickly, we have assumed nobody out there received any kind of message from us. That may not be true. They may have heard Jethro's actual words, or perhaps just a few of his words before the radio died. Or perhaps they didn't hear words at all, but they heard some sort of radio signal. Maybe they heard a phrase like "coast of Maine." Who knows what they heard. However, if they did hear anything from our broadcast and they sail into this part of the ocean there would still be no way for them to know our exact location. I suggest we should have a bonfire going on the beach twenty-four hours a day. Then any ship that sails into our part of the ocean would see smoke during the day and perhaps flames at night. That would bring them here to explore the cause even if nobody heard our call. If we can make a big fire and keep it going twenty-four hours a day, someone is bound to see it or smell the smoke. They will want to find out who or what is causing the fire. It should get someone's attention. We must be close enough to the coast that eventually someone will be affected by the smoke. The bonfire, that's my idea. What do you think?"

"I think it's good, a good idea. Good going, Zoey. I'm not sure why we didn't think of it earlier. I am sure Dad and the others will agree. The only possible problem is convincing The Believers. I know we need their permission. Without it, they might get in an uproar if they saw us starting to build a bonfire. Who knows how they might react. Have you noticed, their attitude toward us has changed. They used to act like we were some species of super heroes, but since the radio failure our status has dropped a few pegs. Jethro and Isaiah have been pleasant enough when I see them, but I think they worry that if they spend too much time talking with us or being seen to socialize with us, it might contaminate them in the eyes of their community. We can't just start building a fire and spring it on them. Jethro is a very practical guy and I'm sure he will see your idea is workable and might produce good results. Why don't you go talk to him and I'll try your idea out on Dad."

"Thanks a lot. I get Jethro to convince and you get Dad. You must admit, you gave yourself the easy job."

"Well, it was your idea. You should be the one to sell it to them. Jethro is a bright guy. He'll see the value in your suggestion."

Zoey gave me a full report of her meeting with Jethro. It didn't start quite the way she expected. She said she was nervous when she knocked on his door. The door opened and Jethro's wife stood before her, a puzzled expression on her face. The two women had certainly seen one another before, but had never actually met. Zoey stuck out her hand anticipating a handshake. Sarah knew the woman standing before her was the daughter of the leader and wondered what she wanted. Reluctantly she offered her hand. As their hands met Zoey gave one of her widest most ingratiating smiles and introduced herself.

"Hello, Mrs. Smith, I'm Zoey Johnson, John's daughter. I'm so glad to meet you. I have met your husband. He seems like a wonderful man. Actually, I came today hoping to speak with him. I have a suggestion that might be of interest to him."

"Well, he's not at home. He's almost never here at this time of day. I expect you can find him at the Meeting House with the group of men who like to sit around, discussing and debating all day long. You can usually find him there. I hope you're not coming to him with more ideas from those leaders of yours. The last idea didn't work out so well, did it?"

Zoey said she was somewhat taken aback by the woman's negative response, but was determined to be positive and friendly herself. She also knew it was important to be as diplomatic as possible. It would not pay to create hostility between herself and Jethro's wife. "It is too bad the radio they tried to put together didn't seem to work the way they hoped, but it was worth a try. The idea I want to suggest to your husband today is my own idea. I haven't even discussed it with my father yet. I wanted to get your husband's opinion first." She sensed the woman's attitude softening.

"I'll be glad to hear your idea. Why don't you come in. I was just about to have my late morning cup of tea. Perhaps you would like some."

"Yes, that would be lovely, but where on earth do you get tea? And, without electricity or gas how do you get hot water?"

Sarah chuckled. "Why, from our tea nursery of course." She paused a moment to enjoy the look of genuine astonishment on my face. "I know when you people got here they must have given you a tour, but you can't have seen everything on our whole island. When the original Believers settled in here and started exploring they came to a part of the forest that smelled like tea. They tracked the aroma to an acre or so of tall bushes, some ten and twelve feet high. The leaves on those bushes had the definite smell of tea. They plucked some leaves, put them in hot water and were happy to discover it really was tea. They experimented with the leaves, and then, in time, our farmers learned how to cultivate and grow our own smaller tea plants. Since then, we have kept the tea plants growing and we have an ongoing tea nursery. As for the hot water, the first thing I do every morning when I get up is pour water into a pot and put it out where the midday sun will bake it. By late morning it is hot enough to make tea. This is one of our few luxuries here on the island. In the middle of Winter we just make a fire in our fireplace and hang a pot above the fire." While she spoke she carefully placed several small green leaves in the bottom of a cup for Zoey and then poured in hot water. Zoey sipped and was delighted with the strong fragrance and delightful flavor of the tea.

"This is wonderful. Thank you. It is really a lovely treat."

Sarah was all smiles seeing her guest's happy reaction. "Now tell me about this idea of yours. I'll give you my opinion before you go to see Jethro."

Zoey decided there was nothing secret about her idea and explained exactly what she had in mind just as she had in talking with me earlier.

"What a marvelous idea. Of course, that's what should be done. Sooner or later, someone is bound to want to know where the fire and smoke are coming from. We should have done it years ago. Jethro and the others are always so worried about the trees. I'm sure they're right that the trees are important, but cutting down a few each day to make a fire won't hurt our forest. There are thousands of trees. How very smart you are young lady. If you have any other ideas come and share them with me first. We can be allies and present our ideas to our men together."

"That's an interesting idea. Maybe we will. I'm so glad we met. I like the idea of the two of us being allies. For now, I think I had better tell your husband my idea and see whether he will give us permission to build a bonfire. I think we should start building it as soon as possible."

Zoey was pleased Sarah seemed so enthusiastic about her idea. She felt that was her first effort at diplomacy and hoped she would be equally successful when she broached her idea to Jethro. When she opened the door to the Meeting House, she saw that Sarah was right. Jethro was there. So were Isaiah and Horace, along with several other men she hadn't met. Zoey told them her idea and explained the advantages of a perpetual bonfire, how it was almost certain to bring people curious about the fire and the genesis of the smoke. She was pleased to see that all three of the Believer leaders listened carefully and appeared interested. When she finished her short sales talk, Jethro was the first to respond.

"It sounds like a good idea, young lady, but let me take a little time to consider the ramifications before I make a decision." He paused for a second, clearly intending to say more when Horace interrupted.

"Jethro, while you're considering her proposal I want to remind you how valuable our trees are to us here. We cannot afford to denude the forest. As long as we continue to live on this island those trees provide everything essential to sustain our people. I agree her plan does sound likely to attract attention, but there is certainly no assurance that it will. We may be so far removed from the mainstream that nobody will ever see the fire or smell the smoke. If it fails to attract attention we will still be living here with much of our forest depleted, it will be a disaster for our people."

Jethro thanked Horace for his opinion and then turned to Isaiah. "I think we should start gathering wood right away. Thank you, Zoey. I can't imagine why we didn't think of such an obvious solution on our own long ago. Jethro, we can have men go through the forest and pick out the trees that look like they are less healthy, and that will require culling in the near future anyway. We'll try to use only those, but if we have to cut some healthy trees as well, so be it. We have a huge forest and the number of trees we might take to make these fires will be a drop in the bucket."

Then Isaiah turned to Horace. "It seems to me you said there was absolutely no need to keep any of those boxes we've had in storage all these years after your group completed their search for parts for the radio. Am I remembering correctly?"

Horace grudgingly replied "Yes, I suppose that is right, but unless this fire produces results very quickly we will still wind up having to cut and burn a huge number of trees, many more than we would normally have to cull."

"There you go again, Horace, always wanting to put a wet blanket on a good idea. While one team is out selecting trees for cutting and burning, we can have another go into the back rooms of the meeting house and finally empty the place of all those left-over boxes of junk from the ship. We can pile them up on the beach as kindling for the fires. Getting all of those boxes out of there and carrying them down to the beach will take some time and manpower, but it will get us started on our fire building much faster. And that will certainly reduce the number of trees that might have to be sacrificed."

Jethro turned to Zoey. "Thank you so much for coming to us with this your excellent suggestion. I am not certain yet how we will decide. You need not waste your time standing around here while we wrangle back and forth about this subject."

Zoey was disappointed she had not been able to get a favorable resolution before she left them, but realized there was one more thing she could tell him that might push Jethro to the correct decision. "Thank you, Jethro. I'll be on my way. Oh, I nearly forgot, Sarah asked me to tell you she thinks the plan for a bonfire is a good one."

"Sarah? What has she got to do with this?"

"I went to your house looking for you. Sarah and I got to know one another. She's lovely and very friendly. She even insisted I have a cup of your wonderful tea. So, we started talking and naturally I shared my plan with her. She's the one who told me where to find you."

Two days later Zoey and I observed teams of the Believers lugging heavy cartons from the meeting house down toward the beach. It was hard work. Zoey had further confirmation her idea had been adopted when we all started hearing shouts of "TIMBER" as trees were being felled all over the forest. Not only had they adopted Zoey's suggestion, they apparently wanted to do it alone without any help or even suggestions from us.

We watched a huge amount of material going down to the beach. The work went on for several days before they were ready to ignite the bonfire. Cutting and lugging trees was backbreaking and time-consuming work. For each tree they cut down, they first had to trim the branches or it would be too cumbersome to move. Once they were trimmed, the trimmings were dragged to the beach where they were further cut down to become kindling. After the branches were taken care of, the tree trunks were cut in half, and teams of six to eight men carried, pushed and tugged the logs down to the beach. They worked hard and long for several days.

The day of the inaugural lighting was a ceremonial and religious event for the Believers. Zoey and I, and a few of our friends watched from above the beach. It looked as though every one of the Believers was down there on the beach offering prayers for success. During the prayer session, a small group of men working with flints and striking stones over wood shavings, ignited several small fires in different sections of the huge pile massed for the initial bonfire. Cheers went up as the big pile started to flame. After a few minutes all the spectators and the fire builders had to back off the beach because of the extreme heat. A short time later they moved further back as the massive fire was generating an enormous amount of heat.

Zoey and I backed away but continued watching from a distance. "Zoey, it looks like that fire is getting much too big. It's out of control. They can't get near it."

"I know! but it's too late to do anything about that now." They watched in dismay as the fire travelled from one pile of stacked wood to another and then another and another of the piles which had been stored on the beach for future fires. This fire was growing larger and more intense than anyone could have imagined. Soon there would be no stored wood left for the next day and the day after as those piles would already have been consumed by the flames.

As we watched, the situation went from too hot, to being out of control, to actually being disastrous. One of the wooden piers caught fire. The fire on the wooden deck of the pier burned to a crisp and then the tops of the support posts burned until the fire sizzled down the posts until it reached water level. The water boiled around it. Fortunately, the second pier was far enough away from the blaze that it didn't catch fire. We watched from our position as long as we could, but no matter how far back we moved from our original viewing post above the beach, the heat became impossibly hot, too hot to stay.

"Oh my God, they count on those piers for fishing. They're going to blame me. It was my idea. We should have paid more attention to what they were doing. We should have insisted that one of us supervise what they were doing or at least advise them."

"I don't think they wanted any advice from us and would have resented it and us if we insisted on telling them what to do."

The fire burned for two more days, and as it burned it generated a great deal of smoke. When it finally burned itself out, smoke and stench from the fire permeated the entire area, making breathing a challenge. The wind that had raged across the beach so fiercely the day of the fire lighting had deserted the area, leaving the smoke hanging in place over the entire settlement. There was no wind at all. If there had been even a breeze the air would have improved some. The beach was black and ugly. The one remaining pier was singed, but relatively unharmed. It was clear nothing would look or feel the same for a very long time.

People remained in their cabins, where the smoke was less intense. Our family, the last family still in the tent, closed the flaps as tightly as possible, but found it ineffective to keep out the smoke. We're all coughing and wheezing. Zoey and I decided we should all move farther away from the area, further into the forest, and make do as best we could. I suggested this to Dad. Dad was still Dad. And he needed to be consulted on all family decisions.

"Yes, I think it will be better to get as far as we can from the smoke. Carl and Zoey, before we actually leave, you've got to tell all of our group. Let each of them decide what is best for their own families. Some of them may want to join us. This smoke will dissipate eventually and we should be able to come back. I am going to speak with Jethro, and tell him our plans, such as they are. I haven't seen or spoken with any of the Believers since smoke started sending people escaping into their cabins. I'm going to look for him now. I hope he doesn't blame us entirely for this mess. His people didn't use much sense the way they set up that fire, and I suppose it will be natural for them to want a scapegoat."

Dad gave me a run down on his meeting with Jethro.

First, he tried the Meeting House. He looked inside and could tell at once there was nobody there. He did notice the treasure trunk still sitting in the middle of the floor, and wondered if that was really such a good place for it. Next he knocked on Jethro's door. He expected to be invited in, but Jethro stepped out instead. He had a cloth mask over his mouth and nose.

"Good morning, Jethro. That mask looks like a good idea. Does it really help your breathing?"

"Yes, it helps some. John, I know this smoke is not your fault. It wasn't anyone's fault. If I were you I would take your whole group as far away as you can get. People are pretty riled and they are looking for someone to blame. I've heard people actually muttering threats against your people. Make sure that daughter of yours stays out of sight. She is public enemy number one. They've pinned the blame on her. I'm afraid my Sarah is responsible for that. Before the fire was built she gave Zoey all of the credit. She told everyone the whole thing was Zoey's idea. She was telling everyone how smart Zoey is. They haven't forgotten it was her idea. For her safety, keep her away as long as you can. People do stupid things when they are upset.""

"Make sure you take enough water with you and whatever else you need in supplies. Good luck, John. I know you'll be back in a few days. Hopefully, things will have cooled off by then."

Chapter 21
Carl

A Ship at Last

We were desperate when we left for the forest. The ten of us walked all the way to the base of the mountain and settled there. Dad said if the air quality didn't improve soon we might have to consider going back onto the ledge and climbing around to the far side of the mountain. The smoke would certainly be a minor issue there if it was an issue at all.

We stayed away for two full days. On the morning of the third day, we all agreed it was time to return to the settlement. We knew the smoke would still be dense, and breathing would continue to be compromised, but it couldn't be as bad as it was when we left. And hunger was driving us. We were just about out of food. We hadn't taken much when we hurriedly left and very little of that remained.

There was really no choice involved. We had to go back, even though we were all concerned about what kind of reception we would face. Dad, Hank and I were most concerned for Zoey. We worried about how people would view her and, more important, how she would be treated. It would be so unfair if they blamed her for the disastrous fire and horrid smoke. To be sure, it was her idea, and her idea was a good one. The Believers' leadership not only liked her idea, they plunged ahead without any kind of planning. If anyone was to blame it was them, not my sister.

It wasn't such a long way from the base of the mountain back to the port area. We had done it before and knew it was little more than a half hour walk. That day, the walk felt much longer. Mom and Dad were moving slowly. They seemed to be having more difficulty dealing with the smoke than the rest of us. We stopped frequently for the two of them to rest. I felt like crying when I watched them plodding along, struggling to keep up while gasping for breath. They were normally both so strong. It was particularly hard to think of Dad suffering just from the effort of walking. He had always been so in command of every situation. It had been painfully obvious over the course of those few days that he was no longer the dynamo he always had been.

As we advanced toward the port area, we were unsure of what conditions we would find. When we were still quite a distance away we could see and hear a surprising amount of busy activity. People were no longer sheltering in their cabins. It was still smokey, however, the air quality was far better than when we left. It was clear enough for us to see individuals at a distance. Surprisingly, most of the people we saw seemed headed down toward the beach. We followed their lead, and saw a crowd gathering on the beach. When we reached our favorite rocky overlook we saw people starting to put together the makings of a new bonfire. The entire beach was charred and ugly from the massive blaze a couple of days earlier, but there was no doubt that they were in the process of building one again. We could see people gathering charred bits from the old fire and throwing them onto the new. Most of the people down on the beach were not actually working. They were looking out to sea. Some had climbed onto the remaining pier, and were excitedly shouting and pointing. It was then that we could see what had them mesmerized. There was a ship out there, a ship still far off on the horizon, but it was surely coming our way!

James happened to look our way and came rushing towards us, right arm outstretched. "Welcome back Johnsons! Congratulations, Zoey! Your idea worked. This terrible smoke surely is what is bringing that ship to us. They are surely looking for us.

Everyone knows it was your idea. Two days ago, some people were blaming you, and now you're a hero! We've been watching that ship since it was first spotted at dawn. It was just a dot on the horizon first thing this morning. It has been coming our way very slowly. It's been slowly methodically inspecting the coast line, looking for the source of the fire."

We stood, riveted to the spot, watching along with all of the others. We could see the ship had come close enough to make out people on the deck. I was happy to see an American flag flying above the bridge. I was surprised to find that the sight of that flag filled me with a sense of pride. I saw it was not a cruise ship or a freighter. It was a military boat of some kind, hardly large enough to transport many people off this island. When the ship was just a couple hundred yards off shore, we watched their activity as they dropped anchor and then lowered two rubber boats over the side of the ship.

There were four uniformed men in each of the rubber boats. The boats weren't very large, but their outboard motors made quite a racket, rising to a crescendo as they approach the pier. Most of the crowd had backed off toward the beach. Jethro and Isaiah alone remained on the pier to greet the newcomers. I was a little disappointed to see none of our people there in the group welcoming the long-awaited rescuers.

The Coast Guard men tied their small boats to a pier post, climbed out and, joined by Jethro and Isaiah, came down from the pier where they were immediately surrounded by an excited crowd. They were cheered as conquering heroes. Jethro, Isaiah, and Horace clearly intended to lead the newcomers toward the Meeting Hall. The path to the Meeting Hall was so jammed with people that their progress was difficult and maddeningly slow.

I realized that that would probably give us time for a break. I suggested that our family ought to head back to the tent so our parents would have a chance to rest before we actually met and started talking with the Coast Guard. I was certain they would be coming to talk with us. As we reached our giant tent, we were met by the entire group of Serenity's senior members. My expectation of time for a rest period disappeared. All those assembled wanted to be part of meeting with the officers. It was obvious to them, as it was to us that Jethro was bound to bring the officers to meet with us after their own initial conference was over. I knew my parents were not going to ignore their friends and go in to rest. Lively conversations started immediately and continued non-stop, as we all awaited our turn with the military men.

I anticipated the officers and their entourage would be headed our way in a short time, half an hour perhaps, or forty-five minutes at most. Time passed slowly as we waited. Finally, two hours later, we watched as they emerged from the Meeting Hall. As they all headed our way I could see only six Seamen rather than the eight who arrived. They must've left two men in the Meeting Hall to guard the treasure chest. The joyous spirit that had been evident on Jethro and Isaiah's faces when they greeted the guardsmen on the pier, and while they were walking toward the Meeting Hall had disappeared. It was upsetting to see Jethro looking positively glum, as he led the group of six uniformed men in our direction.

The air quality was still very smokey and Dad was clearly not breathing easily. Before the newcomers reached us, Dad asked our group if it would be all right with them if I was spokesperson for the group. There was a murmur of agreement. Now I felt uneasy, knowing the meeting might turn into a negotiation crucial to our future.

Jethro introduced the two officers, Lieutenant Phillip Greene and Lieutenant Dexter Lewis. They apparently were referred to as Lieutenants, but Greene was superior to Jones. He had a slightly fancier set of golden braids on his blue uniform. I assumed he was the head man. Jethro Introduced us awkwardly, naming us as visitors from another island. That was not exactly the way I would have described us, but I decided not to clarify our status at the moment. I let them know I was the designated spokesperson for our group. I shook hands with Lieutenants Greene and Lewis.

Jethro rather rudely interrupted, addressing Dad with his own introduction of the newcomers. "It seems dealing with the US Coast Guard may not be such an easy thing. Can you believe, they asked to see our papers! I didn't know what they were talking about. They wanted to see papers they called passports." Jethro looked pleadingly toward Dad. "John, you know our story. You know we have no papers. We have no passports. I don't understand what he was talking about. Our people were all born here. Tell the man. There is no way we could have any official papers. You know that."

Dad stood up straight as an arrow. I was proud of him. His resilience was amazing. I knew how tired he was just moments earlier and how much of an effort it must have been for him to even breathe evenly in that moment.

"Lieutenants, I'm sorry I didn't really listen to your names. Forgive me. The air is not so good and I'm having a little trouble dealing with it. We, that is my friends and I, have been on this island for several months now. We were washed ashore on the other side of the island in the midst of a storm. Clearly, neither I nor any of our people have first-hand knowledge of the history of this island, but we certainly have not seen any officials of the American government or any other government in our brief time here. Jethro and Isaiah have kindly shared the history of their people on this island with us. The current residents here are third and fourth generation descendants of the people originally ship-wrecked here ages ago. I don't know the exact year, and I don't believe they do either. But it seems those who were on that ship were all American citizens from the State of New Hampshire, and all were members of a religious group called The Fellowship of Believers."

"Jethro and Isaiah told us this history and had no possible motivation to deceive, I'm sure this is a true history. Though I have known them only a few weeks, I know them to be men of sterling character. I'm not sure what the issue is with papers, since all of them were born here. There are no government officials on the island, and there is no way they could obtain such papers. I believe the citizenship of their ancestors should suffice to prove them American citizens by birth. In addition, even without any papers, they were born on this island and that alone should be proof of citizenship, since I assume this island is part of the State of Maine. My recollection of American law is if you were born in America, you are an American citizen."

The two Lieutenants listened patiently through Dad's recitation. The one called Lieutenant Greene responded to Dad. "Thank you Mr. Johnson. I find it very interesting that someone apparently as new to this island as you are is called upon to give us the history of the long-established residents. Of course, Jethro had already told us much of what you just said, but it was good to hear it from you as well. Sir, I don't for a minute disbelieve anything Jethro told us and I thank you for supporting the information he gave. It's just that the proof of them being Americans, entitled to come back to America, is perhaps a little more complicated these days because of the political battles on the subject of immigration going on in recent years. It is possible a few years ago they would have been automatically judged residents and citizens, but today they might be judged immigrants, subject to our new immigration laws. As for this island, I am not aware whether it is or is not part of the United States. Unfortunately, that is the way we must view their application for admission at this time. They must produce proof of their citizenship. Sir, we have been discussing with them the kinds of proof they will need to provide to the Immigration authorities. They now understand this."

"Now, Sir, I would like to ask you a few questions about your group, which I understand is about fifty people, including several young children."

"I would be happy to answer any of your questions, but right now I am so tired I would like to sit down and leave it to my son to answer whatever questions you might have about our family and our group." Greene murmured something that sounded like a yes. That was my cue. I told him who we were, and how we came to be there. He nodded his head knowingly when I explained to him how the rising water level had overwhelmed Getaway Island, forcing our evacuation.

When I related how we actually got here on homemade rafts in the storm, he seemed incredulous at first. He seemed more than a little doubtful when I told him about the wonders of Getaway Island before the flood, and how we had all come there as if we were starting a short vacation, and why our families remained on our wonderful island for years. He kept shaking his head in wonderment, but ultimately he must have believed me.

"Well, at least your parents and older members of your group apparently came directly from the state of Maine to that island of yours without actually having left the country. If any of you folks have your US passports with you, even though they are outdated, that will be proof enough of your citizenship and we can arrange your transportation home. Of course, you will still have to stop at Immigration, but that will just be to update information for the record."

I was quite certain none of them, including Dad, would have gone on a two-week vacation to Maine with their passports. But I thought I had better go through the motions. I turned toward Dad, Gunnar, Harry, Mal, Sam Westfall and Joe Brownstein. One by one, each of them shook his head from side to side. Then Mal spoke up.

"None of us have passports with us because we knew we were not leaving the country when we decided to come to an unchartered island in Boothbay Harbor. When we left home it was for a vacation for a week or two. The fact that we stayed there so long was only because we loved life on our island as much as we all did. The fact that we were trapped by the water level making our bridge disappear was a reality we learned to live with."

"We're all Americans. You can ask us anything about America, and we'll be able to give you the answer. For example, if you ask about baseball, I know all about it. I followed baseball all my life before we got to the island. When we were still home, my family were all Yankee fans. That young Italian boy DiMaggio was having a hell of a year when we left. The war was over and all the star players were back. It was going to be a great baseball season. My friend Joe Brownstein here, he's from Boston and in all these years he hasn't stopped trying to convince me that Ted Williams is a better hitter than DiMaggio. I don't know if the others are baseball fans or not, but our two families certainly were and still would be if we had some way of following the games. See, I wouldn't be able to tell you stuff like that if I wasn't an American. You know that's true."

"Thank you. I do believe you. I believe all of you, but you're going to need something a little more official than your baseball story to convince the immigration people that you are US citizens."

I listened to all of the back-and-forth discussion. I was not sure I liked their attitude. I now understood why Jethro looked so downcast coming to us from the Meeting Hall. It was my turn to speak up. I knew I had the answer for these two coast guard guys.

"Sir, every one of our families came from America. We lived in different cities, and we all lived in particular neighborhoods. Supposing each of our senior members here gives you their address when they left home. Surely the cities and towns will have records which can verify their residency. Our folks would not have all lived in those places for years if they weren't

Americans. That will require some phone calls from someone back in your headquarters to check out each one of our families. When they all are verified that should satisfy the immigration people."

The Lieutenant, who had been very serious until that moment, actually smiled. "Why, yes, young man. I think that would do it. Another thing, even easier, would be if some of you folks can show me your American drivers' licenses."

I watched each of our family leaders give a sigh of relief. And Mal spoke up again. "I do still have mine. I knew there was a reason to hold onto my wallet all of these years. My license is in my wallet."

Dad spoke without getting up. "Yes, I'm sure we all kept our licenses and our wallets even though we had no use for the money in them. They're probably all water logged and the print might not be as good as new, but I believe you will be able to read where each of us came from."

The Lieutenant appeared to be satisfied and suddenly seemed to be in a hurry to leave. "Thank you. It has been a pleasure meeting all of you. Right now, we should get back to our ship. I will have to radio all of this information to headquarters. First, they have to know the fire is out and there were no casualties caused by either the fire or the smoke. It was the smoke that brought us here. We were not aware of any groups of people in this general area. We have to let them know about all of you, and get instructions. I want you to understand, our small ship is simply a Coast Guard Response boat. We don't have room for passengers. I'm sure they will send cutters to take you back to the mainland."

"The other matter we will also have to tell them about is that astounding chest full of treasure you people have sitting in the middle of the floor of that meeting building. The story about finding that chest in a ship that has been under water for fifty or sixty or seventy years may be hard for them to believe. I'm sure they will want me to talk with the people who actually found that chest to verify that is how you have it. It looks to me more like a pirate's treasure chest than anything a religious group would have brought with them on a cruise. I'm leaving two of our best men to guard the treasure overnight and until we receive instructions about how to treat what looks like pirate's treasure."

I was about to assure him that the treasure is not ours and we have no claim on it when Jethro broke in angrily. "How dare you question our honesty and even the safety of our valuables. That chest has been sitting unguarded for weeks with no concern for its safety. There is nothing to worry about from our people, not from the people who have been living here all the time it has been sitting where it is."

This was beginning to look as though it could easily become a hostile confrontation between us and our rescuers. "Jethro, I'm sure he is just being super cautious. Government officials always have to play safe. He does have to tell his bosses about the treasure. I don't think he meant to offend you or any of us."

Greene spoke up. "Sorry if you took offense. We simply have to put guards on an your unguarded treasure chest. If I failed to do so, I might be subject to a court martial. Please accept my apologies if it sounded as though I disbelieved or didn't trust any of you. I'm sure you're all telling the truth, but you know we are not the ones who make final decisions. Assuming I can reach the proper authorities, I'll see you all tomorrow in the morning. But it could be as much as two or three days if I have trouble contacting the people I need to reach." With that, the four uniformed men started down toward the port. We watched them until they boarded their ship.

Chapter 22
Jethro

Preparing to Leave

Several days passed without word. Finally, we saw a much larger boat headed our way. We waited on the pier. I didn't want a big crowd to greet them this time. We had serious business to discuss. Of course, Isaiah and Horace were there with me. We watched as the boat pulled in and tied up to the pier. The Lieutenants Greene and Lewis accompanied by two seamen, climbed out. We shook hands all around, and then we headed off the beach and back toward the Meeting Hall.

Lieutenant Greene did not say anything about what was on all of our minds until we were seated around our conference table. Then it was as though he was on the attack and we were the enemy. I've never seen anything like it. When we get this all squared away, I would like to report him for his lack of human decency. I have no idea who to report him to, but he should be reported. No matter what he found out or what he thought he knew about us, we certainly did not deserve to be treated any way but courteously. I expected Horace to get excited as he sometimes does, but when Greene was through with his initial information blast it was as though Horace was in shock. He sat rigid, waiting for the next blow.

The first words out of Greene's mouth were aggressive. "I

want you all not to say anything until I finish telling you some things you may not want to hear. For the past three days we have had people doing research on everything you told us, and there are questions about every aspect of your story. The most important area of concern was the history of your so-called religious group, your Fellowship of Believers. Nobody's ever heard of a religious group by that name. Our researchers could find no record of such a group anywhere. You told us there were Fellowships all over New Hampshire, but that the largest center was in a lightly populated in area in central New Hampshire. You mentioned the towns of Grafton and Danbury, New Hampshire. Investigators went to those towns and nobody there had ever heard of a group called the Believers or any other group called Fellowships. Our investigators made a wider circle, including the towns of Wilmot and Andover, New Hampshire, and got the same result.

"We tried everything possible to find evidence to support your version of your history. We tapped the academic community. The towns you told us about are close to Hanover, New Hampshire, home of Dartmouth College. They have a prestigious history department. We enlisted their aid. We asked researchers in their history department to give us all they could find about a religious group called The Believers Fellowship. Their report was there was no evidence of any such group ever located in or near the named towns or anywhere in the entire state.

"Since we had already enlisted the Dartmouth research

department, we also asked them to check Native American tribes and tell us whatever they could find out about a small tribe called the Huchon Tribe. I'm sorry to say, they could find no record of a tribe by that name or any similar name. So, you see, we have been very thorough in trying to find evidence to support the history you related to us.

"Now Jethro, I know you are upset. Believe me, we bear you no ill will. We do not think you lied to us, but bear with me and think about what I am going to suggest to you. As I recall, you said you are the third or possibly fourth generation of your people on this island. Has it occurred to you that perhaps the original ancestors who wound up on this island with no obvious way off the island and no way for anyone to check what they said, made up this elaborate story you told us. Perhaps they decided they would never be able to return to their old life and they determined to change their entire way of living. At the same time, they created a new history to support the new lives they intended to live, as a God-fearing religious group. They made up the whole religion and created an entire fictional history to relate to their children and grandchildren. The story you told us was a wonderful one. Your parents believed it, passed it along and, of course, so did you indeed become Believers.

"You may well doubt what I am telling you. Why, you may ask, would they make up such a story. Our researchers thought they created that story about the religion because they had a real history they wanted to erase; one they were not so proud of. What I have told you so far has been based on meticulous research. What I am going to tell you now is speculative, but the research people are convinced there are circumstances that support their theory. They have a theory they are planning to check out.

"I know you will not want to believe this and I don't blame you, but they speculate you folks are descendants of a band of notorious pirates. Apparently there were many pirate ships operating along the New England coast in those days. The most notorious of those was led by a pirate king named Henry Avery. Unlike most pirate gangs who had hideouts along the coast, Avery's gang, when they were not at sea plundering peaceful ships, were known to travel inland and to have a home in central New Hampshire. Their home base was rumored to be quite close to the towns you told us were at the center of your Fellowship in that era. The Avery gang was known to have used a Mica Mine in Grafton, New Hampshire as their hideout, the place where they came to live a life of luxury, months at a time. It was the place for them to enjoy their riches when they were not at sea."

As we sat there listing to him slander us, attempting to destroy everything important in our lives, we were stunned into silence. I could hardly stand listening to the man, but he kept on and on.

"Generations of pirate hunters and history buffs have tried to find both Avery's descendants and also their treasure chest which was rumored to have more than a million dollars-worth of jewels and cash. That value was estimated in the early 1900's. Fortune hunters have recently started digging for that chest in and around that Mica Mine in Grafton, New Hampshire as well as in several inlets along the Maine coast. The researchers seem convinced the boat your people were on was not a cruise ship. They are planning to send an underwater team to examine it as soon as we clear this island of people. They will check its design and will be able to certify its heritage. They expect to find it was just the kind of ship used by the pirates of that era, which will mean the people on it were in fact pirates. They had their treasure on board and were off to plunder other ships when they were hit by a fierce storm. Their ship went down. Fortunately, they were close to shore and almost all of their gang survived along with a good deal of their supplies and equipment.

"Why the treasure chest was deliberately left in the sunken ship remains a mystery to the researchers looking into this. Perhaps they thought it would be safe there and they could retrieve it any time they wanted. But here they were on this island with no way off and nobody to contradict any story they wanted to create. The governments of several nations are delighted you nice folks finally brought that chest out of the depths.

"We have been ordered to take all of you people into temporary custody, while we transport you all to Boston to the Immigration people. The term custody sounds harsh, but it really is meant for your protection. We are told you will be met in Boston and questioned by a group of professors from Harvard University and Dartmouth College. I perhaps should not have told you all that I have, but now you at least understand why you are going to be questioned further.

"When the Head of the US Immigration department heard the researchers' theories he concluded if their theory turns out to be true you cannot possibly establish American citizenship; not if you are descendants of pirates. He told us the pirate ships that plagued our New England coast were never manned by Americans. Their crews might have had a few Europeans, but were primarily from Southeast Asia. Of course, this is also speculation, with no actual proof. One of the most prestigious researchers is convinced that rather than a mix with American Indian blood, as you supposed, instead your Asian heritage is why many of your people are on the small side and why some people seem to have Asian facial features and complexions."

Despite all of the upsetting theories we had to listen to, Greene had some good news for us, too. For one thing, they would be taking us off the island. He said they would send a large cutter for us, and transport us to the Immigration and Naturalization Office in Boston. He was told that they considered our possible Pirate heritage to be more probable than not. That was a horrible development and we hoped to fight it. The American authorities said that if it was true, our ancestors were on American soil illegally and none of their descendants could become American citizens simply by having them as ancestors.

They did agree, none of us could have personally committed any of the crimes attributed to our pirate ancestors. That being the case, though we were not eligible to become American citizens, they would do their best to assist us in locating a country willing to accept all of us as a religious community, and would expedite the necessary paper work. He said that after they heard our story, they had sympathy for our plight, and hoped they could help us fulfill what he called our dream of going to Greenland.

An unfortunate side issue came up. Several news reporters got wind of our story and decided to make it into a scandalous front-page spread. They called for a Congressional investigation of us as possible agents of some foreign country. They headlined the treasure in the trunk, and insinuated that we must somehow have obtained it illegally.

We did get some important good news, too. I suppose the best news of all was that someone in the United States State Department decided we needed a champion on our side to do battle with the bureaucracies. He hired a lawyer to represent our various interests. The lawyer he hired was from a highly respectable Boston law firm, Sullivan, Sullivan, Peabody and Cohen. Our lawyer's name was John L. Sullivan. Apparently one of his ancestors was a boxer, actually the Heavyweight Champion of the World named John L. Sullivan. Our lawyer was named for a fighter.

Lieutenant Greene said our John L. Sullivan had already stepped in the ring for us. He immediately contacted the Danish government about us. We learned Denmark administers Greenland as being a part of their country. He hadn't yet gotten a yes or a no from the Danes about us moving there, but he was encouraged because the Danish government had a policy of promoting immigration to

Greenland as a way to increase both the population and productivity of that huge, largely unpopulated, land mass. There was no guaranty, not yet, but it was encouraging.

As for the treasure chest, Sullivan told both the Coast Guard and US Immigration and Naturalization Service that they had no right to hold it, since it was in our possession when the Coast Guard illegally removed it from the island. Sullivan filed papers, asking for a declaratory judgement from the Massachusetts Superior Court. He asserted that the United States had no direct proof that the belonged to pirates, and since it was in our possession, it was rightfully ours. Sullivan felt that we had a very good chance to win that suit and the treasure should be ours. Unfortunately, while that suit made its way through courts, the chest would be held in escrow in America until our ownership was finally established.

It was uncertain that we would wind up in Greenland. We didn't know for sure if we would get to keep the treasure. What we did know was that we were going to Boston for a time, and hope we'll be fortunate enough to meet you people there as well.

When we leave here, it sounds as though you Serenity people will have to wait for a different boat. Through our new lawyer's connections, we have been promoted to priority status by the Coast Guard. Greene did say another cutter will come to take you people home.

Chapter 23
Carl

Home at Last

Later that day, the entire Serenity Cove group sat above the pier and watched as four seamen carried the treasure trunk from the Meeting Hall, and slowly made their way with it down to their ship. Mom, Dad and the other senior members were waiting with their drivers' licenses in hand for inspection by the Coast Guard.

After meeting with the Believers, Lieutenant Greene and his team came to meet with us. Zoey and I joined with our parents and the other seniors for that meeting. It went smoothly. The drivers' licenses were shown, and Lieutenant Greene proclaimed that our parents were certainly US citizens and that made us citizens as well. The Coast Guard would be sending a smaller cutter in a few days to pick us up and take us to Boston or any other Northeast port we choose. We looked forward to being welcomed on the cutter and understood that we would be taken to Boston to meet with officials there to verify our citizenship. After which, each family would be on its own to decide where they wanted to live. We didn't know exactly when that would happen, but Greene led us to believe it would only be a matter of a few days. Then it would be up to each of us to try to rebuild our old lives or start to create new ones. For the first time in decades, we didn't know what that meant for our community.

We all agreed that it was time for a Serenity Cove meeting to make sure that we were all on the same page regarding this promising situation. After we were sure of the facts, we became nostalgic. Wherever we settled, we agreed to meet one year after our Boston landing, and have a reunion to relive all of those wonderful years we shared at Serenity Cove as well as the more recent perilous times here on the Believers Island.

Collectively, we were concerned that our hosts, the Believers, despite the seemingly favorable turn of events, were still in for a much more difficult path. However, that was the path they had chosen, and they were all excited to be leaving this island, their hearts being set on being allowed to settle in Greenland.

A few days after our Serenity Cove meeting, Zoey, Hank, Mom, Dad and I were back sitting on that same rock above the port, spectators to the arrival of the promised large cutter which would carry the Believers to Boston.

A different set of officers came off the boat. Neither of the Lieutenants, Greene nor Lewis was with them. We watched as our friends Isaiah, Jethro, Horace and James were there to meet them. We all went down to the beach to say goodbye and to wish them good fortune. They had treated us so well in our misfortune and now they were off to an uncertain future, all of their beliefs and understanding of who they were had been shaken to the core for each and every member of The Fellowship. Were they really descendants of pirates or of a rather noble band of Believers? They might always wonder, but to us they would always be The Fellowship of Believers. We waved goodbye, and stood watching as they boarded the ship. There were tears in many eyes. They were all leaving the home that had been theirs all of their lives.

Then they were all gone and we were alone on Believers' Island. To us, it will always be The Believers' Island just as we will always be from Serenity Cove. Like the Believers, we also were three generations, but on this island we are just accidental visitors. Mom and Dad, and a couple of others from their generation were starting to show their age. It was sad to think that some of them wouldn't be with us for too many more years. We were alone now, on the island in the middle of 'nowhere'. We had fifty-four cabins at our disposal, a large meeting hall, a work shop, a pier for fishing and possible future boating. We had fishing equipment, a vegetable farm, a tea garden, a proven water source and lots of tools and equipment. As our family sat around contemplating the future, Zoey was the first to say it.

"You know, if we could somehow get electricity and telephone service to this island, it's really an ideal place to live."

It was just a thought, an idea to bounce around. We discussed the difficulty of getting electricity and telephone service. "Don't you remember, at Serenity Cove we didn't have telephone service. We didn't have electricity either, not reliable electricity. Nor did we really miss either one. We had full days and went to bed early. Remember what it was like?"

Dad said, "I remember very well. I loved every minute of it."

Mom nodded in agreement. We all chimed in with our own happy memories. Then we talked about what it would be like to stay here, on Believers Island and make it happen all over again.

Then we started thinking of the challenges, problems, and issues. It turned out, according to the Coast Guard charts, the island was about five hundred miles North of Boothbay Harbor and far distant from the coastline. It seemed unbelievable that we had somehow managed to get tossed and thrown five hundred miles north of Boothbay Harbor on that terrible day. We were much farther North, much further out to sea, subject to far more severe winters and impossibly far from emergency help. The Believers were always worried about the winter that was ahead. They said some winters were so hard that if they hadn't had their strong faith in the goodness of the Lord they would not have survived.

On Believers Island we didn't have insulated buildings, fireplaces or even winter clothes. We could probably get a modern two-way radio to connect with the mainland. But of course, it would have to be delivered by boat. It could be many years after those cutters sail away before any other ship comes near here. Yes, it might take years before we could get electricity. It initially was fun to think about and fun to talk about, but then we got more serious in thinking about the future.

This was when Mom, quiet until then, vehemently joined the discussion. " I hope you know all that talk about staying here is just nonsense. We all loved Serenity Cove, but we didn't have any real winter. John, I'm sure you remember when we would look out and see snow falling off in the distance and marvel that it could be possible when we had spring-like temperatures at Serenity Cove.

"This island is so much farther North. The winter weather will be even worse. I shiver when I think of being cooped up here in the winter. I can imagine my feet freezing in the middle of December and not thawing out completely until the first warm week of March. I can see us all huddling under blankets days at a time. Can you picture Dad and the other men trying to shovel paths between the cabins and coming in with frozen hands and pants frozen stiff as boards. It's time for us to stop dreaming. It is time for us to go home."

"Our grandchildren have never seen America. They have no idea how much they have missed in all of our years away. They have never gone to real schools, seen a movie, watched television, or tried out for a team or a school play. We have been so isolated from the real world for so long we have come to think of this world as normal. It isn't and it never was. It is time to go home." I knew she was right. It really was time to go home.

The cutter that came to pick us up was smaller and more intimate than the one which had removed the Believers a few days earlier. The captain of our ship was another kind of Officer, Lieutenant Commander Theodore Frank. He also turned out to be an affable, relaxed kind of officer, not a bit officious. He asked us to call him Ted. We enjoyed long conversations with him. We regaled him with much of our history, recent and otherwise. He seemed fascinated by our description of Serenity Cove.

We all enjoyed the luxury of the cutter. Among other things, there was television. It was certainly a novelty to all of us. Many of our group planted themselves in front of the TV set for hours at a time. They couldn't get enough of the constantly changing views of the world on the screen in front of them.

The weather was getting warmer that day as we travelled south toward Boston. It was notably warmer the following morning. "Captain, where are we now?"

"We've covered quite a few miles. We're getting close to where you all started. We'll be outside Boothbay Harbor in less than an hour." I went out on deck to take in the scene. I knew what I was looking for, but I wouldn't say it out loud. Most of the others moved out as well. We were all hoping to see our Getaway Island one last time.

"Look, there it is!" Everyone ran to the starboard side. "I see it now plain as day, there's the Golden Gate Bridge just ahead near the coast."

"Captain, captain! Can we stop the ship? Can we get closer to the island. Yes, that's our island we told you about. That's it! That's Getaway Island!"

The captain checked his navigation maps. "I certainly see the island out there all right. But I'm checking my chart and there is no island there. That's funny, these charts have all of the islands. How could the cartographers have missed it? I do believe my eyes. I see the island and I see that marvelous bridge you told me about. If you want to get closer, we can take you right to shore to have a look. I might even come with you."

Half an hour later we were all in rubber motor boats heading toward the island. Each boat had a sailor driving. The captain was on board with our family. When we pulled in to the small beach, Dad, Gunnar and some of the others seemed puzzled. "Why does it look as though nothing ever happened here? You remember, all those cars that floated off the bridge, and the line of cars on the beach and the road, all were swallowed up by the sea? When the sea level went down, they should still have been sitting there. Where did they all go? They couldn't just disappear. Could they all have just floated away? We speculated about the missing cars and the people in them. Finally, we just gave up, and accepted their disappearance as something we would never comprehend.

At Dad's suggestion, we held a short memorial service dedicated to all of our friends who disappeared that day, our deliverance in the face of the terror and death of so many of our friends from Serenity Cove. We had watched as their cars slipped off the bridge, as the water rose overwhelming those still stranded on land.

"I urge us all to take a few moments to think about and mourn the loss of so many we knew for years, some of whom we loved. They were all our friends, people we worked and played with through the years. Now we think of them as gone and lost forever. Let us each take these moments to think about them, those special friends who were part of our lives, part of who we are. Let us take this time for prayerful remembering. A remarkable silence followed as each of us thought back to that day and painfully remembered.

The captain, who was standing with us on the beach, was eventually the one who broke the silence. "I'd love to see that dream place you all told me about. Is it too far a walk?"

"I'm not sure all the old people will be able to make it that far on foot." Dad heard me and pretended to be insulted. "Young man, if you can walk that far, so can I. I just might take a little longer getting there."

We started walking. We made quite a parade! It was a long and tiring walk, but nobody suggested stopping. The captain was right along with me at the front, becoming more and more excited at the prospect of getting there. Finally, we came to the dirt road with the sign announcing "Serenity Cove" still hanging slightly off kilter on a tree, just as it aways had.

We walked down the driveway to the familiar clearing. It all looked so familiar!! We didn't expect to see anybody, but there was a woman waiting to welcome us. She looked pleased, and not at all surprised to see us coming. She reminded me of Ellen. But obviously, it couldn't be our Ellen. That would be impossible. So were the words out of her mouth, impossible but wonderful to hear.

"Here you are, at last! Welcome back! You are a little late, and we were beginning to worry about you. Dinner is ready and we have all of your favorite foods. Just go and wash up now. Your cabins are ready for you. Dinner will be on the table when you come back. After dinner we will have time to catch up on all that has happened while you have been away."

The End

Author's Note

I had great fun writing this story. I started with the idea of a family going off on vacation to a magical island. My intention was a short story of the family set on the island. However, once I got them there, I started to wonder how they would ever get off the island and where they would go from there. As I answered those questions the entire story came to me, complete with unlikely twists and turns. From there it was just a question of getting it down on paper, hopefully in an entertaining manner.

After I had written the first few chapters I asked a friend, Cynthia Keenan, if she would like to read what I had written and comment. She read faster than I could write, so I had to work furiously to keep writing ahead of her reading. Her encouraging comments, didn't always agree I was on the right track, but she was always very diplomatic. Thank you, Cynthia.

After I completed the first draft my son, Robert Sharenow, read the entire manuscript, and made a dozen valuable comments and suggestions, almost all of which I adopted in revisions. His most important observation was the need for me to make clear to the reader who was narrator in each of the chapters. His input was enormously helpful.

Sue Krevlin, my daughter, has become my most valuable writing assistant. She started as helpful proofreader, but soon elevated to unofficial copy editor and finally to editor. She scoured my manuscript not only for typos, but in addition made numerous suggestions which helped modernize some of my "old fashioned" language. She also designed the striking front and rear book covers. A simple thank you does not quite cover all she contributed, but thank you, Susan for your time, effort and various skillful contributions.

Most of all, I thank Judy, my wife and lifelong partner, for her support and encouragement all through the process. Her suggestions are always valuable. There were days when she would patiently listen to third and fourth re-readings of the same sections, as I tried to iron out issues which inevitably come along.

My thanks, as always to Michael Pastore who has demonstrated great faith in me as a writer, giving me encouragement to keep writing. His company, Zorba Press, specializes in books about education, children, and summer camps. My book was clearly well outside of those areas, but he enthusiastically agreed to publish it.

About the Author

Arthur Sharenow spent sixty summers of his life in camp. He started as a camper at a very young age and continued on in camp until his retirement. He experienced every aspect of camp life, from camper to counselor, to Unit Leader, to Head Counselor, and finally to Owner/Director. After selling the camp to one of his former outstanding long-term camper-counselors, he stayed on for an additional eight summers so he could continue to enjoy the sheer joy of being at camp, a place always alive with the excitement of childhood and youth.

"I loved being a camp director. How many people are ever given the opportunity to try to create a perfect world. We Camp Directors have that opportunity every summer. A perfect world for our campers was always my goal. Many summers we came very close. Other years we fell somewhat short. The summers that stand out in my mind as most collectively challenging were the last three summers of the 1960s, where the national turmoil associated with the Vietnam War spilled over into summer camps. Happily, the mood of the country changed in the following years, and we experienced decades of wonderful camp seasons.

"After my retirement from summer camping, two new interests became prominent in my life. I took a number of writing courses, several of which were writing memoirs. Many of my memoirs turned out to be camp stories. My writing instructor encouraged me to turn those stories into a book, which I did. **37 Summers: My Years as a Camp Director**, is a collection of memoirs, all from the pages of my camp memory.

My previous book, The Summer Camp Uprising is a novel and comes from the same memory source, but is entirely fictional.

"My second new area of concentration was photography, re-awakening an interest from my early teen years. I worked hard at photography, learning and doing. Eventually I started exhibiting and selling the photos I considered my best. Along the way I started teaching photography, and have been doing so over the past dozen years. What I like most about teaching photo classes is that it reminds me of coaching kids in softball and baseball, something I loved doing all of my adult years at camp."

About Zorba Press

Embraced by the gorgeous gorges of Ithaca, New York (USA), Zorba Press is an independent publisher of paperback books, hardcovers, ebooks, audiobooks, and YouTube channels.

Zorba's mission is to promote the innovative ideas and the daring books that inspire creativity, nourish children and childhood, humanize technology, point the way to a renewed culture of love and kindness, courage and freedom, sincerity and peace.

For more information and a complete list of our current published works, visit Zorba Press online at

https://ZorbaPress.com

About Zorba Editing

Zorba Editing (like Zorba Press, a division of Zorba Media) provides the complete range of editing, writing, and publishing services for authors, students, businesses, publishers, and content creators.

https://ZorbaEditing.com

Also Published by Zorba Press

37 Summers: My Years as a Camp Director
a memoir by Arthur Sharenow [ISBN: 9780927379373]

The Summer Camp Uprising
a novel by Arthur Sharenow [ISBN: 9780927379526]

Camp Counselor Smart Guide:
How to Work With and Play With Kids at Summer Camp
by Michael Pastore [ISBN: 9780927379427]

Kids Play Games:
101 Active Games for Happy Children
by Michael Pastore [ISBN: 9780927379458]

Lark's Magic: a funny novel for children
by Michael Pastore [ISBN: 9780927379076]

Child Maintenance:
How to Respond to Misbehavior Without Force, Rewards, or
Punishments by Michael Pastore [ISBN: 9780927379434]

101 Problems in Child Maintenance:
Real-Life Training Situations for Everyone Who Works With
Kids   by Michael Pastore [ISBN: 9780927379380]

Visit Zorba Press online at https://ZorbaPress.com

www.ingramcontent.com/pod-product-compliance
Lightning Source LLC
Chambersburg PA
CBHW020639260626
47157CB00008B/2815